Praise for *The Train of Salt*

"Richly poetic, a significa[n] ... literature."
Paul Ash, *Sunday Times*

"Compelling ...epic and cinematic. Nothing of Hollywood here, as this story, the central love story—beautifully handled, tender and sombre—helps to consolidate the novel's major concerns. Azevedo is masterly in pacing his narrative. The tension is implacable, but there are brief lulls and pauses that stave off reader exhaustion and prevent the novel's hold from short-circuiting ... it offers outstanding commentary on the fracturing and violent reconfigurations of a community under civil war. Transfixing ..."
Chris Dunton, *Sunday Independent*

"What an enthralling story and what great storytelling ... a fascinating, eye-opening account of the atrocities committed by soldiers on both sides during the bloody Mozambican civil war. Yes, it's a story of blood and tears, but it's also a story of courage, love and an indestructible will to survive. Great, great story."
Lucas Ledwaba, *City Press*

"This is a harrowing, emotional journey."
Arja Salafranca, *The Star* **Tonight**

"A remarkable story that relates the tales of ordinary people during the horror of war."
Drum **magazine**

"... a bitter-sweet, poetic exploration of humanity trying to survive the brutality thrust upon it by war."
Kelly Vos, www.buffalocity.net

"Incredible ..."
True Love **magazine**

"A moving and poignant story."
Sunday Tribune **Christmas Book Guide**

"Heart-rending ..."
Soul **magazine**

"... has the gritty realism of a story based on experience."
Marion Whitehead, *Getaway* **magazine**

Published in 2007, reprinted July 2008 by
30° South Publishers (Pty) Ltd.
28, 9th Street, Newlands,
Johannesburg, South Africa 2092
info@30degreessouth.co.za
www.30degreessouth.co.za

First published in 1997 in Moçambique by Ndjira
as *Comboio de sal e açúcar*

Copyright © Licínio de Azevedo, 2007

Translated from the original by Mugama Matolo

Design and origination by 30° South Publishers (Pty) Ltd.

Printed and bound by Pinetown Printers (Pty) Ltd., Durban

ISBN 978-1-920143-12-1

The Train of Salt and Sugar

Licínio de Azevedo

Translated by Mugama Matolo

30° South Publishers

Foreword

I first encountered this book approximately five years ago at the Maputo Airport. As an avid collector of anything related to the railways of Mozambique (and there is very little in print on this subject), that there was a book dedicated to the Nacala Corridor came as quite a surprise. In my case, the result was that it is the only novel that I have ever read from cover to cover in the Portuguese language.

Since then I have from time to time encouraged those involved in publishing in southern Africa to bring the book to print in the English language, the logic being that it would open to a much wider audience the story of the Nacala Corridor during Mozambique's civil was. I would like to thank in particular Paul Ash for his work in bringing the book to the attention of 30°South Publishers. We are grateful for the opportunity to support the book as a sponsor.

Railways are, among other things, rich in history and this book brings to light the critical role that CFM North played in not only serving, but keeping the region alive during those troubled times. We stand on the shoulders of those who preceded us; with this book their sacrifices are acknowledged to many readers for the first time in the wider world outside of Mozambique.

Henry Posner III
Chairman
Railroad Development Corporation
Pittsburgh, Pennsylvania, USA
www.RRDC.com

RDC RAILROAD DEVELOPMENT CORPORATION

Licínio de Azevedo is a filmmaker and writer. He arrived in Mozambique in 1977 and worked for the National Film Institute researching stories of the Mozambican liberation war. His first book, *Relatos de Povo Armado* (Tales of the Armed People), recounted real stories from the Moeda Plains in the north of Mozambique—the first region to be liberated during the war, and became the basis for Mozambique's first full-length feature film. He has worked closely with such renowned filmmakers as Ruy Guerra and Jean-Luc Godard. He worked with the Social Communication Institute for five years, and produced the award-winning educational television programme, Canal Zero. He lives in Maputo and is co-founder of the film production company Ebano Multimedia.

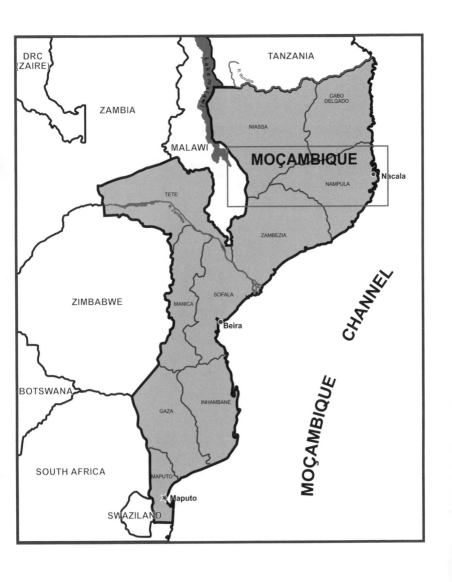

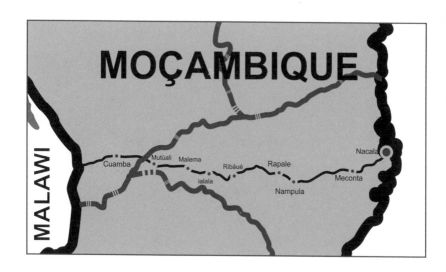

"A dead animal does not choose the knife."

—Makonde proverb

Nampula Province, Moçambique, circa 1987

Like an expressionless eye, the Nampula station clock does not indicate what time it is. It has been like that for a long time now. But, anyway, it is not important. The day, which is today, of the departure of the three trains that will leave in a column, has already been determined. Just not the time. In the faint light of dawn, around the dense shadows of the trains, the restless forms of the escorting soldiers and the barrels of their rifles can be distinguished. More difficult to see, however, are hundreds of other forms that are gathered, sitting on the ground or lying on their straw mats near their bundles on the station platform and its dimly lit surroundings.

This 'secret' departure, the preparation for which started about five days ago with the organization of the three trains, attracted everybody's attention almost immediately. It has been impossible to conceal the fact that the escort is being assembled, because the soldiers themselves have been spreading the news among their relatives and friends. Even more difficult to hide is that the employees of the Supplies Department of the Northern System of the Railways of Moçambique have been buying large quantities of 'Celeste' maize meal, cooking oil and dried fish. The whole city has become aware that these products are for feeding the soldiers and the train crews, the twenty permanent railway workers who will be accompanying the convoy of trains.

Many people have been sleeping at the station or in its surroundings, anxious not to lose their places, which they have been vigilantly guarding ever since the departure of the last train almost three months ago. Their numbers have been increasing constantly and, even now, there are many others who are arriving with their bundles. Like silent ghosts, they do not make any noise as they plod through the potholed tarred streets of the sleeping city, accompanied by relatives who will not be travelling but who help carry the bulky bundles and buckets of water. They barely talk, saying the minimum when they pass through the gates of the station that are guarded by armed militia. They say little when they are subjected to the compulsory searches. Even when they walk along the stony courtyard while searching for a space on the platform to settle among the crowds, they talk in low voices. To talk about what? The essential need to travel? To once again try and convince oneself that it is worthwhile taking the risk? To comment again on what happened during the last journey, when almost all the occupants of the train were killed or kidnapped?

For several years now, since the war started spreading throughout the region and the enemy began diverting his attacks from the road to the rail system, the trains stopped hauling passenger cars. Now, the only closed wagons are those for cargo and the conductor's van at the rear of each train. The rest are O.I.s, meaning 'open irons', according to railway terminology, and simply called 'irons' by those who travel in them. They consist of a platform with sidewalls that are one-metre high and are usually used for the transportation of bulk materials and are less comfortable than those used for animals. The multitude that is waiting to embark and travel in the 'irons', unsheltered at their own risk and account, is not made up of passengers in the true sense, since *Caminho de Ferro de Moçambique*—CFM, no longer issues tickets. This ceased when the war began claiming its own price, in lives. Those who are travelling, exposed to all risks in order to reach their destinations, are the *povo*—the 'people' who will act as the labour force to repair the sabotaged railway line.

৯৯ ৯৯ ৯৯

Mariamu, a stout and strong-willed woman, endowed with a youthful beauty still visible despite her thirty-five years, is worried. She rises from the straw mat spread on the platform that she shares with a sad-eyed woman of the same age but without the same energy. She moves a few steps away from her companion and the bundles and becomes distinguishable in the motionless mass. She stops in the dark vacuum next to the train. She stands quietly, observing the wagon that is carrying her luggage, a few metres away from where the platform ends. What worries her is a group of soldiers, one of whom is holding a torch and peeping through the wooden slats of the wagon, trying to ascertain what is inside. The soldiers are suddenly summoned by an officer to install an 'anti-air', an anti-aircraft gun, at the rear of the train. Calmer now, Mariamu returns to her place.

The journey hasn't even yet started and they already want to know what's the cargo, she murmurs to the companion.

If it's not them, then it's the others who are going to steal from us, says the companion resignedly. *It's pointless trying to do any business on this route.*

With the fifteen bags of salt that I'm carrying, I'll buy about twenty bags of sugar, Mariamu says.

Obviously! If they don't steal them ... if you manage to reach

Malawi ... and if you return.

I'll manage to sustain the family for a year. Sugar is cheap in Malawi. I know how to calculate. How much is a kilogram of sugar here in Nampula? There isn't any—even for tea!

Do you know that they bury the dead near the tracks in the bush, without prayers or anything?

Then, why do you travel? I have seen it all. I know how it is.

Oh! Why do I travel? Just like you, I have children and also I don't have a husband!

You're becoming a superstitious old woman. Didn't you bid your farewells correctly? Didn't you leave the ancestors satisfied? Then? They won't let us die far away from home.

C onductor Omar Imuli, forty years old, with a prematurely aged, round face, hair completely white and a short beard, comes out of the station and walks across the platform toward the trains, dressed in his impeccable blue uniform. During this journey, he is the chief conductor, responsible for all three trains and, as such, will travel together with the commander of the escort in the conductor's van of the last train. He passes near Mariamu, who is his neighbour in the quarter where he lives.

Excited, she stops him. *When's the departure, Mr. Omar?*

I'm going to have a chat with the commander to find out if the soldiers are ready, he answers. *It's no longer the stationmaster who gives the order to proceed, but them.*

Who's going to travel at the front?

The mine detector is—One One Zero One. The conductor indicates the train in front of them, the one carrying Mariamu's sugar. He vaguely points to the side that is masked by 1101 and, soon afterward, far behind, at the workshop area, explaining, *One One Zero Three will follow and the last will be One One Zero Five.*

Why all these long numbers? Mariamu asks. *The train to Cuamba used to be One Zero One.*

They're extraordinary trains. No one knows when they'll arrive, Omar explains.

Nor if they'll arrive at all, the other woman adds.

Who's the commander? asks Mariamu.

Seven Ways, Omar replies.

Oh! With him, we'll arrive! she exclaims.

Y es, we'll arrive, muses the conductor when he resumes his walk toward the workshop area. But when? How long will they take this time to travel the three hundred and forty-one kilometres to Cuamba, where they will be substituted by another crew that will take the trains up to the border? One month? More? The train crews nowadays subject themselves to the unpredictability of the journeys with the same discipline of the old days—those times when there was no war, when they would attempt to get the old trains, which were first hauled by North American and later by Brazilian locomotives, to adhere to the timetables. These days, a journey is a 'punishment', according to the language common among them. Omar was 'punished' about twenty-four hours ago when, together with ? of his colleagues, he received instructions that he had osen for the shift. *A dead animal does not choose the knife,*

is what he says. He is an employee and he has to obey. He bade farewell to his wife and five children, his eldest fifteen years old, solemnly but without any sense of tragedy. After all, the five per cent extra salary that he receives for each day spent during the journey to and from Cuamba corresponds to what he earns in a year. Closeted in his bedroom, he had read some portions of the Koran and had secretly sent one of the children to buy a five-litre jug of firewater made of fermented paw paw. He respects his religion when he is in the city but when he is on the train he needs the firewater to calm his nerves in the dangerous sectors where there is never any shortage of sabotage and attacks.

When Omar reaches the rear of 1105, Commander Seven Ways is giving instructions to his assistants who are all standing next to the conductor's van. The commander is thirty-five years old. When speaking he holds a wildebeest's tail which he shakes in the air with one hand and with a fist raised to chin level as if to reinforce his words. Tucked into his belt are a Makharov pistol and a small axe that resembles a fire-fighter's. Around his neck is a whistle which looks like a football referee's. Lieutenant Taiar and Second Lieutenant Salomão, commanders of the escorts of 1101 and 1103 respectively, listen to him in silence.

Omar gives the officers a wide berth to clearly show that he is not listening to what they are discussing and he enters the conductor's van. He goes into his personal compartment, a comfort that the conductors and the commanders will enjoy as privileged occupants of the van. He calmly sits on the bed and waits for orders. He knows Seven Ways' habits and has more faith in him than the other commanders. If there is anyone who can take them to their destination and back, that person is Seven Ways. He is not an ordinary commander who bases his actions only on facts or suppositions about the enemy's actions, on military tactics or on his guerrilla experience against the Portuguese, but he has a pact with the spirits. According to him, there is no logic, either military or civilian. There is a magical relationship with the universe, whose efficiency in military terms surpasses the clearest and most brilliant logic. Omar has shared the compartment with the commander on numerous journeys. The commander is polite in his day-to-day dealings with everybody but ruthless with the enemy. He never refers to his magic. During combat, the order is only one: *No one flees!* It is said that when he was young, during initiation rites, he was injected by the Makonde traditional healers with a mixture of roots of certain trees and the hair of a lion, which he himself had killed, armed only with a spear. As if this were not enough, inside his wildebeest's tail, which has been relieved of meat and cartilage, are secret drugs which have been stuffed in to render him invulnerable.

We are ready, Seven Ways' voice interrupts the conductor's thoughts. *We are leaving now.*

Omar rises and stands to attention as if he is a soldier. He has become so accustomed to receiving orders from Seven Ways, instead of commanding his own train. He communicates by radio with the station saying that they are ready. He also contacts Adriano Gil, the train driver of 1101, in which the only other radio is installed among the three trains.

Without having been told by anyone, but as quick as lightning, the hundreds of people who are waiting to embark start running toward the trains and occupy the 'irons', sitting on top of the cargo and the thousands of sleepers that will be used to repair the sabotaged railway tracks during the journey.

⁊ ⁊ ⁊

Mariamu goes to 1101, the train that faces the greatest risk since it will be in the front … the mine detector train. She wants to sit next to her salt and guard it during the journey. The companion, who has twenty cases of empty cool-drink bottles, which she will exchange for full ones in Malawi, prefers to travel in the third train.

Side by side, Lieutenant Taiar and Second Lieutenant Salomão walk silently toward their trains. Taiar is twenty-seven years old. Salomão is twenty-nine and will soon be thirty this coming March. He is lean, a little taller and slightly curved. With a long beard that gradually becomes sharper from the chin downward, like a billy goat's, and with a glaring look, he seems to be another Rasputin. Taiar is strong and proportionately built, possessing a handsome face that is almost beardless. He walks upright, with a natural elegance. They walk together for the two hundred metres between the conductor's van and the 1105 locomotive and part without speaking to each other as if there were an invisible train separating them.

In 1103, Salomão jumps into the 'iron' that is almost completely occupied by a fishing boat with a covered cabin and painted bright yellow and red. It is destined for Lake Niassa. Like a child fascinated with a new toy, he has decided to install his command post in the boat instead of the conductor's van.

Taiar passes 1103 and makes his way toward the locomotive. It is already dawn and the sky is clear. He lights a cigarette and looks at his Russian watch, given to him by his Ukrainian girlfriend at the end of the officers' course that he completed at the Lvov Military Academy in Kiev. The time is half past five. He frequently remembers the Ukrainian even though much time has passed. He has not had a girlfriend for a long time now. Military life only permits casual relationships and for this he has no reason to complain. Youthful, well-humoured and with a friendly voice, he is well known for being a good commander and loyal to his soldiers. When he is in Nampula, Cuamba or Nacala, he always has female company. Otherwise, he does not possess anything of importance besides two or three civilian shirts, a few pairs of trousers and a dark blue suit that he bought during the Fourth Congress of the Frelimo Party —when the shops were completely empty except for a brief period when they were inundated with imported suits.

In the cabin of 1101, sitting on a chair on the left, Stoker Celeste Caravela, a man of fifty with a shrunken face, and a former station messenger who started working on the trains only when he was forty, distractedly reads a Bible. On the right of the cabin, train driver Adriano Gil, thirty years old and with a Cantiflas-like moustache, watches the indicators, the rise in the level of the airbrake pressure.

Train driver! Lieutenant Taiar calls from outside. *I'll travel with you when the journey starts.*

I've already given instructions that a stool should be placed for you, lieutenant, Adriano Gil says. *I know that you like to travel in the locomotive.*

In the 'iron' immediately behind the locomotive and occupied only by soldiers, is the first of the 'anti-airs' which each train carries—to be used against people rather than against aircraft. Taiar sends two soldiers to assemble all the civilians, both passengers and railway workers—the latter filling an 'iron' with their equipment and who will be travelling in 1101. Almost all have embarked and some are already improvising shelters with sheets of cloth and straw mats to protect themselves from the sun. In short time, one hundred and fifty people surround Taiar by the locomotive.

I'm the commander of this train's escort, says Taiar. *When the train stops for any reason other than an attack, no one is to alight without an order to that effect. If it's an attack and when the train stops, everyone must jump from the side that is opposite side of the attack and you must crouch next to the line or look for cover under the 'irons'. If you don't manage to jump, you must lie down inside the 'iron' until the fighting stops. Under no circumstances must any of you flee into the bush—because of landmines—and also because the enemy will be shooting from one side and at the same time covering the other side to capture you. I'm the one who is responsible for this train as well as for your well-being. I don't want indiscipline as I must fulfil my obligations. You're going to be facing a war situation. Many of you must have made similar journeys and you know what I'm talking about. Those who haven't been in a combat situation before must try to be calm. Don't be frightened by the noise of the shooting as this is not what kills. Most of the time, it is our very own fear that brings about our downfall.*

The sun rises behind the station. The building is now visible, modest and without the airs of being the station of a provincial capital and, beyond it on the other side, the street, the Railway Club and a few of the city's taller buildings that are discoloured by the passage of time and by the scarcity of resources because of the war. Everyone quickly embarks except for some of the soldiers who pretend not to be interested in the journey that is about to begin.

Before returning to the locomotive, Taiar goes to the back of the train where, in another 'iron', is half the escort with the second 'anti-air' under the command of a young sergeant. Taiar exchanges a few words with him, also a veteran of the anti-colonial struggle, more out of friendship than of necessity as the sergeant is well briefed on his duties. He has been in the war for a long time but does not have a more senior rank—only because he is illiterate.

The lieutenant sits on the wooden stool that has been placed for him in the cabin, between the stoker and the train driver. *You know the norm?* he asks the train driver.

If I hear shooting, I stop, answers Adriano Gil and the stoker confirms this with a nod of his head.

Celeste Caravela shoves the Bible into the satchel that contains his clothes and, like the train driver, looks outside through the window toward the rear, waiting for the green flag.

Hello Namina Station! Hello Namina, Nampula calling! Hello Namina, Nampula calling! Over! the radio operator repeats his call for a few minutes without the other station responding—it is unaccustomed to the passage of trains.

The 1101 conductor, Patrício Joaquim, having been personally told by the stationmaster that they can proceed, raises the green flag through the door of the conductor's van. Two hundred and fifty metres ahead, the order is acknowledged. The piercing hoot of the locomotive can be heard across the city. The crowd that is waiting alongside the tracks to say their farewells gets excited. The passengers respond to the farewells and settle themselves into their positions. They are already feeling isolated even though they share company with others—travelling toward an uncertain destination—in spite of the fact that they know where they want to go.

Adriano Gil slowly accelerates the two-thousand-two-hundred-horsepower D-123 diesel-electric locomotive, hauling sixteen wagons. A melancholy departure with many sad faces, the crying of relatives and friends who are gradually being left behind, a few dozen metres at first and then a hundred, two hundred metres and then later, somehow, many kilometres.

From hereon the community of 'irons' substitutes the family, the community and the city. Within seconds, a known world disappears to be replaced by another, always unknown—the world of fear. It governs the insecurity of those travelling alone, the anguish of those who are more than alone, the ferocious comradeship of the soldiers and the superstitious conviction of the railwaymen that one never travels with one's relatives since this brings bad luck.

In the confined space of the locomotive's cabin which he shares with Lieutenant Taiar and the stoker, train driver Adriano Gil sometimes feels that he is transporting all these people to their death, that he is not piloting a train of cargo and people but a funeral train ... to an enormous, collective funeral.

Again, a green flag confirms the start of the journey. This time only the stoker receives the order to advance.

We can go! he says.

However, the train does not increase speed but continues at five kilometres per hour, the maximum speed permitted on the journey. Soldiers who have delayed embarkation walk next to the train, passing their weapons—one an AK-47 and another a bazooka—to their comrades already aboard and then they jump onto the 'irons', enjoying themselves, like children.

One soldier stays down by the tracks and pretends to be deserting. *Good-bye! Have a good trip!* he waves at his comrades, laughing. He then runs and jumps onto the 'iron'.

The first curve, precisely just ahead, masks the station from where Second Lieutenant Salomão's 1103 is also leaving, to be followed by 1105 a few minutes later. The trains are separated from each another by a kilometre, all with the same number of wagons and all with almost the same number of soldiers.

Hello Namina, Nampula calling! Over!

Namina here! Over!

Namina, at last! We are informing you that Trains One One Zero One, One One Zero Three and One One Zero Five have departed. They are carrying the Third Company and the order is to clear the way at all costs until final destination. Please inform the other stations. As soon as the trains arrive, please inform us, as usual.

Still within the city, in a low-lying area, a thick mist suddenly appears despite the fact that the summer is coming to an end. The train is almost knocking over the shacks lining the tracks, most of which are in a precarious state, belonging to the refugees. Many people walk across the track unmindful of the train because of its slow speed. A goat escapes from the hands of a boy who has been dragging it. It jumps between the wagons to the other side of the track and everyone laughs as it disappears among the maze of shacks—a moment of distraction for the travellers.

Adriano Gil almost hoots when he nears the suburb where he lives. He looks to his right, at his home that is situated about thirty metres from the tracks and which is made of cement bricks and roofed with zinc sheeting. However, it is not necessary to hoot as two of his children are on their way to school together with other schoolchildren. They wave proudly at him. He cannot see the youngest or the mother. Just when the train is passing, she appears at the door of the house but it is too late to wave.

Neither the stoker nor the train driver notices the deep emotion that makes Adriano Gil want to cry. The lieutenant is looking in the opposite direction toward the city and does not see anything that evokes emotion. Behind some of the two- or three-storey buildings that were constructed in the seventies, and all looking the same, he imagines the Military Cinema Theatre and, farther ahead, the Military College from where he had departed on his way to the 'friendly countries'. He does not treasure any memories of those times—the only memories he cherishes are those of his youth.

Celeste Caravela remembers that today is Thursday. On Sunday, if lucky, wherever they stop they might find an abandoned church. He will then ask the commander for permission to hold a prayer meeting.

The departure information is transmitted from station to station and from station to train. Calisto Confiança, the Iapala stationmaster—the third station from Nampula and located almost half the distance to Cuamba—writes the information on a piece of paper taken from his son's school exercise book. He leaves the station where he lives him, he painted the city red until it had been time for him to go to the station. He still has a half-full bottle left over from the party, a 'true Scotch', which he sips slowly, meditatively. Next week, he will be turning thirty. Yes sir! He is getting old. He must enjoy life more; take advantage of what is good and better. This is urgent as he only has seven years left. It is his ancestors who told him so and he totally believes this. Some sort of serenity engulfs him and he gulps more from the bottle.

The first dangerous spot, known to all, begins at kilometre 232, forty kilometres from Nampula, stretching for the next ten kilometres or so.

Up until around eleven o'clock, they cover twenty-five kilometres. They then come across a section of track of about twenty metres—which had previously been sabotaged and then repaired—in a precarious state because of erosion from the rains. Taiar and some of the soldiers alight and search the area. There is nothing out of the ordinary. The soldiers take up positions in the bush and alongside the train. The permanent railway workers begin working without the assistance of the *povo*. The lieutenant informs the commander over the radio of what is happening.

In less than two hours, the workers manage to repair the damaged section. But from then onward, they have to proceed very slowly because of the bad state of the tracks, so much so such that Taiar decides to walk ahead together with some of the soldiers, followed in turn by the railway workers who inspect the tracks for damage. In certain places it is necessary to stop and move the locomotive manually, wheel by wheel, to force it to pass. The only thing now remaining is to lift its

with his family and walks about one hundred metres to the other side of the road to one of the few shops of the village still surviving the war. Calisto hands the paper to the shop owner, a middle-aged Indian, and returns to the station satisfied with himself. He has a cousin who is an armed bandit, as they are called. The secret, only known to a few, among whom is the shopkeeper, is that he transmits to his cousin detailed information on the movements of trains, the composition of each, its cargo and the size of the military escort.

❧ ❧ ❧

As soon as 1101 leaves the city, the tracks become a tunnel in the grass that is well watered by the summer rains. In the dense bush, the remains of huts and a paw paw or banana tree that has been attacked by termites can be seen here and there, as well as a few rare and roofless, doorless, windowless stone buildings. Farther ahead are some almost completely destroyed buildings belonging to an agricultural company that ceased operating a long time ago.

The stoker and the train driver, though travelling at five kilometres per hour and with their eyes fixed on the ground in front of the locomotive, can hardly tell the state of the track. On the curves to the left, the stoker looks through the window to check whether the train is still complete or if any wagons have come adrift. Now and again, they identify sections of the track that have relatively new sleepers, which in this sector are rare indeed.

This is where they killed Joaquim Hilário, Adriano Gil indicates.

The linesman? Celeste Caravela adds rhetorically.

Yes, the linesman, confirms the train driver and turns to Taiar. *He was up the pole phoning when they shot him.*

Taiar seems not to be listening but is observing the area in front of the locomotive while at the same time half-listening to the conversation between the two. Before he goes back to his soldiers or to his compartment in the conductor's van, he wants to ascertain the morale of those who are responsible for traction. *Traction, indeed! I already use the language of the Railways,* he thinks.

About three kilometres behind, in the conductor's van of the last train and using his bed as a table, Omar Imuli is playing cards with Commander Seven Ways. Religion forbids gambling but it is the military who command here. The commander had appeared with the cards and asked him whether he knew how to play. He could not tell a lie. From time to time, without the need to look outside, Seven Ways talks about the battles, the sabotage and deaths that have occurred hereabouts. Omar asks himself whether the fact that the commander always wins does not mean that he also has the power to guess his opponent's cards. Whether by coincidence or a ruse, the commander loses for the first time.

In the 'irons' many of the passengers and soldiers are sleeping. Mariamu, who is wide awake and with her back leaning against her bundle, is thinking about her children whom she is leaving behind with her sister. What have they eaten today? Have they gone to school? She mentally calculates again how many bags of sugar she is going to buy in exchange for the salt she is carrying and how much she is going to get when she sells the bags of sugar in Nampula. She is satisfied at the prospect of making a profit, very confident of her luck and imagines her children being well fed and dressed in clothes bought in Malawi. In the brilliant sun with the 'iron' shaking rhythmically as if to lull her to sleep, she feels the presence of Carlitos near her. She imagines herself being happy, happiness she does not experience anymore though men are never in short supply. She sighs as she remembers her husband Carlitos, the shopkeeper from Malema, who was captured four years ago and has not been seen since.

When do they attack? During the night or during the day?

The woman next to Mariamu is travelling for the first time. The question drives Carlitos' image away and Mariamu feels like answering her rudely. When she sees the woman's expression of fear, she relents and speaks to her gently. *They never attack during the night. It's mostly during dawn or dusk. But it's always, well ... almost always during the day.*

It means they also attack during the night? the woman asks, more frightened, as if death is more cruel during the night.

No! Mariamu says. *It's during the day. At four or five in the morning when we're drinking tea or at five o'clock in the afternoon when we stop to eat.*

Why? the other asks.

Probably they want to eat with us, Mariamu jokes.

෯ ෯ ෯

Sitting at ease, with his legs supported by the edge of the boat, Salomão is placidly appreciating the scenery. He has decided that today must be a day of rest as yesterday, in the company of a policeman friend who enjoys drinking with

one hundred and twenty tons and place it farther ahead.

At four o'clock in the afternoon, everybody is able to return to the train as the track is now in a better state. They are dangerously close to kilometre 232. *It is a bad time for us to arrive here, so we will sleep with the enemy,* Taiar thinks worriedly as he embarks with his men onto the 'iron' that is armed with the 'anti-air'.

As if reading his assistant's mind, Seven Ways orders the train driver over the radio to stop, the aim being to spend the night there. Adriano Gil obeys, letting the engine idle since he can only switch it off at a station where, in case one of the locomotive's eight batteries goes down, another locomotive stationed in parallel can provide the electric current to restart it.

We will be attacked at dawn, Taiar thinks as soon as he realizes what is happening. *If only we could have accelerated a little more, perhaps we would have managed to get through tonight,* he reckons. However, he alights and starts organizing the soldiers into advanced pickets on both sides of the train, about thirty metres into the bush. They are thinly spread out. The other two trains arrive, almost glued to each other. The three trains together stretch over a kilometre, as if they are one single, immense train. Over the locomotive's radio, Adriano Gil and Celeste Caravela can hear Omar Imuli informing Nampula station of their position.

The people are ordered to alight and quickly prepare something to eat. They offload pots and buckets of water and collect firewood, never venturing too far from the line. Coming from the rear, Seven Ways goes past 1101 with the wildebeest tail in his hand and walks alone until he disappears in the grass that shrouds the track. He is armed only with his Makharov pistol and the small axe. Taiar is not worried because whenever they stop and the area in question is suspicious, the commander will walk ten kilometres off the track on a solitary reconnaissance and return with valuable information.

An hour later and next to the locomotive, Adriano Gil and Celeste Caravela are eating mealie meal with dried fish, placing a pinch of salt and dried chilli in their mouths every time they chew the fish—to smother its vile taste. Seven Ways passes them on his way back from his reconnaissance and disappears toward his train.

I was once a soldier. I know why they generally don't attack during the night, Adriano Gil says to Celeste Caravela.

I've been attacked during the night, the stoker answers.

Yes, but it's rare. They lose the advantage they have during the day of being able to see us while we cannot see them. At night, all of us become invisible.

Even the train, the stoker agrees.

Even the train, the train driver emphasizes.

The sun disappears behind the rocky mountain, which is round like a pregnant stomach with its navel facing the sky, and it soon becomes dark. Seven Ways, once again, is playing cards with Omar Imuli.

Adriano Gil and Celeste Caravela, accustomed to journeys such as this and fully aware that all will very much depend on their own forces, stretch out their straw mats under the locomotive and prepare to sleep. They never sleep inside the cabin as this is the preferred target for the first grenades in an attack. Passengers and soldiers have just finished eating and are also preparing to sleep or, in the case of some of the soldiers, to start their guard duty. Without stopping their game, the commander notes through the open window of the conductor's van that it is dark. He sends his orderly to summon Lieutenant Taiar and Second Lieutenant Salomão. The game only stops when the two arrive. He secludes himself away with the officers for a few minutes in his compartment. The two officers leave hurriedly and Seven Ways informs the chief conductor that they will continue the journey within a few minutes.

Don't talk over the radio. They might hear, he warns.

The enemy might hear? the conductor asks.

The spirits are with them.

At that moment everyone along the trains stirs, surprised by the order to hurriedly embark. Within seconds, Adriano Gil and Celeste Caravela roll up their straw mats and climb to their positions in the cabin.

Don't switch on the headlights, Taiar orders while standing next to the 1101 locomotive, ready to instruct the soldiers still in position in the bush to return and embark.

Along the train, the people are confused, trying to locate their belongings in the darkness. Silent disorder prevails as the soldiers tell them to hurry.

Let's go! Hurry up! the soldiers repeat in hushed tones while pushing, sometimes brutally, those who are not quick enough.

Impatient and without looking, Adriano Gil steps on the yellow pedal, known as the 'dead man', with his right foot as if to confirm that it is still there. When he first heard the name of the pedal, he had not liked the sound of it at all. It is a mechanism that automatically stops the locomotive if and when, for whatever reason during a journey, the train driver removes his foot from it. Thereafter, when he was adept at operating locomotives, he quickly became accustomed to the name and began to like its sound, as if it invoked occult forces. He now philosophically reasons that he and the 'dead-man' are cogs in a wheel that depend on something that is greater that itself.

Taiar climbs up the small ladder of the locomotive and he enters the cabin. *Let's go,* he orders.

A small jerk forward and the train is on its way in the darkness, opening a passage through the grass.

A bit faster, Taiar says.

The order is not to travel faster than five kilometres per hour, responds Adriano Gil forcefully.

The orders are also not to travel at night, Taiar retorts.

At ten kilometres per hour, they cover nearly three kilometres in fifteen minutes and Taiar orders Adriano Gil to stop and switch on the headlights. The powerful light of the locomotive illuminates the grass and they are able to distinguish huge tree trunks placed across the tracks, separated from one another by a few, irregular metres.

Taiar alights running, advancing with a group of soldiers through the tunnel of light that probes deep into the night. Then, guided by the other soldiers and completely unaware of what is happening, hundreds of civilians—men, women, old and young—hurriedly disembark. Obeying military orders, they begin to unblock the track without any idea of the extent of the sabotage. Metre by metre, the train advances.

Eight kilometres are covered by one thousand trunks, each trunk needing the effort of ten people to remove it. It is three o'clock in the morning when the last trunk is finally shifted out the way.

Taiar and his soldiers continue on foot, attentive to landmines or booby traps. For example, they find two sections of track that have been disconnected—enough to cause the derailment of the locomotive, which thus would waste several days, at the same time subjecting them to the dangers of attack.

Noticing that his colleague is sleepy, Celeste Caravela approaches him. *Do you want me to pray loudly in order to keep you awake?*

Adriano Gil is so sleepy that he agrees with the stoker's preposterous proposal. Celeste Caravel begins with the Creed, to which he now and again adds some improvisations. Complying with his religious obligations, he does not forget about his earthly duty of being a stoker, staring fixedly on the track as if his eyes were the train driver's second pair. At times, despite the futility of the effort in the dark, he even glances out to the rear to make sure that the train is still intact. His voice echoes louder than the locomotive and Celeste feels that he is a preacher who has been chosen by the Lord as his prayers are keeping the train driver awake. He is also certain that by constantly scrutinizing the track, since he has been purified by faith, he is able to detect all the dangers ahead—even landmines buried beneath the rails, as if they were serpents sent by the Devil, which the soldiers are not able to detect.

It is a splendid daybreak. They are on a plateau from where they can see miles upon miles of the open plains around them. It is only then, upon Seven Ways' command, that Taiar interrupts the train's movement and orders it to stop. There, several kilometres away from the enemy who had been preparing for a dawn attack at the tree-trunk ambush site farther back, soldiers and railway workers can now rest their exhausted bodies for a few hours. The passengers, completely worn out from the labours of shifting the massive trunks, have long been sleeping, piled up in the 'irons'. Many only wake at midday when the trains resume their procession, this time at the regulated speed of five kilometres per hour.

Hello, Namina! Conductor Omar Imuli calls from his radio in the 1105 conductor's van. *Hello, Namina, reply! Over!*

Namina here! Speak One One Zero Five. Over!

I inform you that we are going past kilometre two six three. Over!

Welcome to Namina!

Be steady, colleague! Six kilometres still remain to be covered.

At midday, they arrive at Namina under the curious eyes of hundreds of people, virtually all the villagers who have come to the station to watch the trains arriving after such a long absence. With emotion, Adriano Gil realizes that they are there to welcome them. In just a little over twenty-four hours, they have covered seventy-seven kilometres, which, during such times, is a record. Other trains have taken ten days to cover the same section due to attacks, sabotage and derailments.

Really, we are well protected, thinks Adriano Gil. *We have Christ in the One One Zero One locomotive, Allah in the conductor's van of the last train and Seven Ways linking us to the ancestors.*

There is nothing particular about the Namina station. It resembles a warehouse with half of the lower part of the green walls peeling off and the rest painted in a dull yellow. Before it, the remarkable Namuli Mountains rise, constituted by huge rocks that accompany the railway line for approximately one hundred and fifty kilometres, always on the left side, before moving away toward the south. Behind the station there are the village shops and a few ruined brick buildings surrounded by huts that belong to the refugees.

Without the discomfort of the noise of the locomotive, Adriano Gil readies himself to sleep under the nearest tree with the satisfaction of one who is returning from a journey—when one leaves the station and walks home, sometimes at dawn when everyone is asleep.

Very few people alight at Namina as there is practically no cargo to be offloaded, except a few trunks and boxes for the local military garrison. In contrast however, a large number of people approach the conductors hoping to embark. They have been here for months with no transport to return to their homes or they are war refugees who want to rejoin their relatives in another village or even in Malawi. They do not feel secure in Namina, which sooner or later is bound to come under siege. The conductors repeat to all of them the same warning: *You travel at your own risk. We do not carry passengers.*

The soldiers disappear into the station's surroundings in search of alcohol and entertainment. A group from the 1103 escort tries to break down the door of a cargo wagon without disguising their intentions. Attentive and standing at the door of the conductor's van, Omar Imuli is aware that he must go to them and impose his authority of being a conductor. It is an attitude that requires courage as the soldiers' reaction is always unpredictable. Before he leaves the conductor's van, he goes to his cabin and gulps a sip of the firewater made of paw paw.

You can't do that! Omar says sternly.

The soldiers are surprised.

I know the military regulations. You're here to protect the train and what it transports and you can't touch the cargo, he states.

Be careful, old man! a soldier warns him. *In the next battle, the first bullet will be for you.*

I'm the chief conductor of these three trains. You write in your report that the wagon was plundered by the enemy but we, in ours, we have to write the truth since we are accountable to CFM for the cargo.

Don't say we didn't warn you, old man, says the soldier who seems to be the leader of the group as he moves away, taking his companions with him. *This old man is mad. He wants to enter into a confrontation with the military.*

We'll whip you! another soldier says, threatening Omar with a closed fist as if he is holding a stick.

One shot. One bullet is enough! the first one adds.

The attempted break-in forces Omar to stay in his conductor's van, now with reinforced vigilance over the cargo wagons.

Having been informed that they will spend the night and leave the following day, the travellers settle themselves in the surroundings of the trains with their improvised kitchens, straw mats and blankets, which unfortunately not all possess. A small market stall of firewood immediately springs up by the station. Many of the passengers visit the shops but there is nothing for sale. The shops continue to operate merely out of formality since they have not been restocked for a very long time, almost since the days of the Portuguese.

In 1103, with an aggressive attitude and indifferent to the looks of the people milling about nearby, Second Lieutenant Salomão is standing in front of a twenty-year-old youth who is stout and beautiful and is modestly dressed, clearly a young city woman.

I'm not going! the youth says firmly.

I'll shoot you, Salomão threatens.

I'm not your wife. I'm not going to cook for you! she screams, pursing her lips and stamping her foot on the ground.

The people nearby pretend not to notice anything and move away. It is better not to involve oneself when a soldier is with a woman. Even then, Salomão screams at her.

Go away from here! What do you want? she protests.

He seizes the girl's arm and starts dragging her towards the 'iron' loaded with the boat.

She resists, determined not to give in. But her efforts are insufficient against the trained muscles and the skill of the second lieutenant.

She does not stop screaming. *Leave me alone! Leave me alone!*

The soldiers watching the spectacle smile as if it is normal for a man to beat his wife when she is disobedient.

That chick needs to be beaten! one of them comments.

It's on the straw mat that the second lieutenant is going to beat her, another says. *He's going to pound the chick, that's what's going to happen.*

Salomão drags the girl toward the 'iron' but she refuses to climb up. For this, he needs more than his physical force and, therefore, he places his hand on the holster.

Do you need some help, Salomão? Lieutenant Taiar asks.

Surprised, the second lieutenant looks at Taiar without drawing his pistol or letting go of the girl who by now thinks that all is lost.

Let her go! Taiar quietly orders.

His command electrifies the air. The nearest soldiers, all from Salomão's escort, stop smiling and watch the exchange with a clear dislike for the lieutenant. The civilians now watch and listen, as if someone has touched the sleepy chord of their courage.

Lieutenant, captain ... nobody gives me orders regarding this woman, declares Salomão, agitated. *I won my rank in combat. Ten years! I've a right to the woman I want!*

While responding to the lieutenant, he lets go of the young woman's arm and she, with dignity, moves a few metres away, awaiting the outcome of the confrontation. Taiar remains calm, silently meeting Salomão's threatening look.

Here, the conversation is that of man to man and it's I who commands in my train, continues the second lieutenant.

Don't provoke me, Salomão, Taiar says without raising his voice, sure of himself.

Two of the second lieutenant's soldiers ease closer in an attempt to intimidate Taiar with their AK-47s. Without paying any attention to them and indifferent to Salomão's expression of scorn, the lieutenant turns abruptly and goes to his train. The young woman runs after him and joins him as he walks.

Thank you for helping me. My name's Rosa. I'd like to come to your train since I no longer feel safe here. I'm a nurse. I can ...

Do what you want, Taiar says without stopping, barely looking at her, without regard for her request.

She runs to the wagon containing her luggage, two medium-sized bags and a white case with a red cross on the side. She grabs them and runs after him with difficulty because of the weight. Still without looking at her, Taiar goes to the conductor's van for a quick sleep.

Rosa walks along the train and, without any particular reason, decides to settle in the middle, in the 'iron' in which Mariamu is travelling.

A couple that is travelling in 1103, having witnessed all that has happened to Rosa, decides also to change to 1101.

Salomão stops them as one passing sentence. *No one changes trains during the journey! From now onwards, each one has a marked place!*

Rosa and Mariamu end up sitting together in the shade of the same tree. It is very hot with a dry, hot wind, like a devil's breath, raising dust all over the station. In the plain that stretches to the mountains, the wind forms whirlwinds with soil and leaves spinning upward in convulsion.

It's said that within the whirlwinds there are witches, Mariamu says.

I don't believe that, answers Rosa, laughing.

A relationship of empathy and comradeship immediately develops between the two women. Rosa tells her about what had happened in the other train.

What surprises me is that no one had the courage to intervene, she complains. *Except the lieutenant.*

And do what when faced with guns? It's the soldiers who command. You're lucky, but at this very moment another one might have been taken by force. Not even the children escape. This Salomão who wanted you is a bandit. He once raped a twelve-year-old girl here in this very station. The mother, on hearing the screams of the daughter, kept on repeating 'She doesn't know how to do it. She's never done it. She doesn't know how to do it.'

Mariamu, like an older sister endowed with the experience of the line and of life, explains to Rosa how to deal with the soldiers—be distant, never look at them. She assures her that she will be safe in 1101 because she knows Lieutenant Taiar. He is not one to abuse anyone and his soldiers are more disciplined than the others, even though they are no saints.

A soldier is like a child, she states. *He always wants to experiment and test his commander and if the commander is worthless ...*

In my case, it was not a soldier. He was a commander, Rosa says. *That's worse.*

The conversation changes direction, both happy in the other's company. They talk about the reasons for their journeys. Mariamu explains about her salt and sugar business and her expectations of profit. She talks about captured Carlitos and about the four children she is single-handedly looking after. Rosa tells her that she did her probation as a nurse in Nampula and is now returning to Cuamba where she is going to work in the village hospital. She was supposed to have stayed for only six months but, because of lack of transport, she was delayed for almost a year. When going to Nampula for her course, she was offered a lift in an Antanov plane belonging to the air force. This is the first time she is travelling by train.

In the afternoon, Adriano Gil and Celeste Caravela are preparing their supper under the locomotive after the stoker had, without success, gone to church in the village which, to his consternation, was closed. The priest had long since fled to the provincial capital from where he flies in a small plane once a year to attend to collective baptisms and weddings.

The sheep are without a shepherd, the stoker tells the train driver sorrowfully.

What sheep⸮ the train driver asks. *Not even goats exist here. They were eaten a long time ago.*

You're a Pharisee, Celeste Caravela is irritated. He threatens, *If you joke about God's matters, you'll see what will happen.*

Omar is still worried about the cargo wagons and therefore he is forced to station himself permanently at the door of the conductor's van. Seven Ways, closeted in his compartment, does not show any sign of life the whole afternoon.

Taiar sleeps for a few hours because he wants to confirm before nightfall that the local garrison is attentive to the station security. He walks along 1101 and, at any moment now, will be sending for his meal that is being prepared in the military kitchen installed in one of the 1105 'irons'.

Seeing him passing by, Mariamu calls out to him, *Good afternoon, lieutenant. What is the army's supper today*⸮

As always, dried fish and mealie meal, he answers, friendly, coming closer without recognizing Rosa but Mariamu. He remembers her from a previous journey when the escort's food ran out and they had asked her to loan them three bags of maize.

Rosa sits by her friend and is busy stirring mealie meal in a pot with a wooden spoon. She is suddenly timid, a thing that is not common to her, and does not remove her eyes from the pot that she is mixing vigorously—more so than is necessary. It is only at the mention of her name that she raises her eyes.

Nurse Rosa is a very good cook.

Oh! The nurse! Taiar recognizes her.

We also have mealie meal, Mariamu announces. *But it is with nhemba beans. Everything is almost ready. You're invited.*

Taiar once more looks at Rosa, this time noticing her beauty.

I accept, he says. *Thank you. I'm tired of eating with men only!*

He calls a soldier and sends him to deal with the escort's food. He sits on the straw mat, which he asks for as if at home. Rosa sits next to him, both leaning against the trunk of a tree, an acacia with yellow flowers.

Strange, he thinks, *I never notice that a woman is beautiful when I see her for the first time.*

The supper is served and they talk while they eat, but there are moments of silence, in part due to the melancholy ending of the day. Taiar looks all the while at Rosa and she, bashfully, diverts her eyes. To hide her embarrassment, the nurse looks at the rocky mountains

I'd like to go to the top one day. Everything must be beautiful when viewed from there.

They are the Namuli Mountains, Taiar says. *Their altitude is two thousand metres.*

It's true! I read that in Geography, she remembers.

It's said that the first Macuas originated from these mountains.

In Cuamba, there are the Metucue Mountains, she says, pleased to find a subject that makes it easier to look at him. *Also, there are many stories about them. Hundreds of people led by Chief Namakoma*

went to live there when the Second World War started.

Afraid of the war?

Yes, running away from Hitler.

Hitler? Here?

All of them knew who Hitler was, just like Salazar. My grandfather told me that they were very scared of him. They thought that the Second World War was the end of the world. So, they fled into the Metucue Mountains. There's never a shortage of water and everything that is planted grows well there. Even this present war does not reach on top there. It's a place of peace.

I'd like to live in such a place.

I've always thought that the military liked war.

That is like saying nurses like diseases, Taiar answers.

She laughs at this observation, showing her perfect white teeth.

I wanted to be an agronomist or a veterinarian, he says. *I like plants and animals.*

I've always wanted to be a nurse, Rosa is also willing to make revelations.

When I completed my secondary education, they selected me to be a soldier. The Motherland needed to be defended. It was the priority—it was during the war with the Rhodesians.

These wars never end.

For one year, I was in the Military College in Nampula and they sent me to undergo a course for officers in the Soviet Union, in the Ukraine. After defeating the Rhodesians, this other war started and I didn't have any other alternative but to continue fighting. But, to me, this isn't life. It's a duty, an obligation.

Ever since I was a child, I've always liked to see nurses with their white uniforms and I used to say to my father that when I grew up, I would be a nurse so that I could wear one also.

When the war finishes, if there's still time, I'll try and study, Taiar promises. *I want to redirect my life in another way.*

Marry, have children ..., interrupts Mariamu who has been quiet, thinking about Carlitos.

A soldier can't get married, Taiar states. *He's married to the army, to the bush.*

ঙ ঙ ঙ

Inside the boat, which belongs to a fishery project at Lake Niassa and which is not all that comfortable but is ideal as a sitting room when compared to the rest of the train, Salomão drinks firewater made of sugar cane from a five-litre jug in the company of some of his soldiers. They talk loudly, all of them a little drunk.

This lieutenant doesn't behave like a soldier, one of them says.

He's always against us, another accuses.

Such a soldier compromises a mission, the first one states.

Yes, if he's captured by the enemy, he reveals everything so that he won't die, a third one says.

Without knowing that he'll die anyway, the first one adds and all of them laugh, contaminated by mournful humour.

He's probably consorted with the enemy since he wants to lower our morale, affirms another. *Have you ever thought about this?*

It's true! To stop us from mobilizing the women.

Our women!

I don't know ..., one hesitates. *After all, if he's a lieutenant, it's because ...*

Lieutenant! exclaims Salomão with disdain. Until now, he has been quiet, concerned only with drinking more. *Just because he has been to a military academy of the Russians? Fighting is learned in the bush!*

And eating the bush! the first soldier states.

Pass the jug, a hesitant soldier asks Salomão. *It's first class.*

I had to smash the guy, boasts the soldier who had sourced the jug of alcohol. *He wanted to sell it.*

Once again, they all laugh, united against the civilian who had not wanted to contribute to the 'upliftment' of the military's combat morale. They pass the jug from hand to hand.

❧ ❧ ❧

Outside the train where Salomão is drinking, a soldier has just opened an AK-47 bullet with the help of a bayonet and is pouring gunpowder into a flask. He shakes the flask to mix the contents and drinks the little liquid that remains. Then, he takes a walk around where the passengers are preparing to sleep and, like a dog sniffing a bone, he carefully examines all the women, old and young. He decides on a woman lying on a straw mat next to her husband, both still awake and alert.

This woman is mine! the soldier says, pointing at her.

Which one? What? The husband is afraid.

Suddenly, the husband tries to rise, to react, but he is knocked to the ground with a rifle butt to his head. The soldier moves away, dragging the woman behind him and disappears in to the darkness.

❧ ❧ ❧

Have a good rest. Tomorrow, we're going to enter a dangerous area where there's no shortage of attacks, Taiar tells Rosa and Mariamu when he says his farewell. *The most important thing is to remain calm. Please, don't forget.*

During the night, Taiar wakes up a number of times and comes out from the conductor's van where the conductor Patrìcio Joaquim is sleeping in a compartment next to his, to inspect the guards. He does not trust the local commander—he is too given to drinking. Cannabis is free while alcohol has to be bought and, since the soldiers are always broke, they resort to violence and exacerbate relations with the civilians.

On one of his walks, the lieutenant comes across Salomão who, being very drunk, moves as one who constantly stumbles over his own shadow. On recognizing him, Salomão tries to give the impression that he is walking straight but it is useless as he no longer has control over his body. He holds onto the 'iron' with his right hand so as not to lose direction, now and again touching his pistol as if to ensure that he has not lost it.

༺ ༺ ༺

I n the light of the moon, the Namuli Mountains shine in the night as if they are majestic witnesses to all that is happening in this particular region of Moçambique where the war is very intense.

If all the people were to die in the war, would the Makuas reappear from the mountains? the lieutenant asks himself.

A small wind, announcing a change in the weather, suddenly blows for a few seconds like the passing of a bad spirit or a wandering demon without the patience to cause mischief. Taiar is not used to sleeping much and enjoys walking at night when most people are asleep. As it is relatively safe, a few small fires are still alight and people talking in low voices can be heard. A child cries out briefly, perhaps from hunger, and he concludes that the mother must have given it her breast since the crying suddenly stopped. He passes where Rosa and Mariamu are sleeping and where other people have gathered, trying to mutually protect themselves in their sleep. He stops and observes them for a few seconds and tries to imagine what all those people, sleeping together, are dreaming of. Aimlessly, he continues walking while he thinks that perhaps one person's dream interferes with the dream of another who sleeps nearby and that the combined dreams form another bigger dream, without an owner and as free as the inhabitants of the Metucue Mountains that Rosa talked about.

⚘ ⚘ ⚘

The warm wind of the previous day has driven the good weather toward the sea. The new day takes time to come, with a sky that is covered by dark clouds. Around the fireplaces, the passengers are preparing tea without sugar—a product that the war has made scarce in this region, distant as it is from the production centres of central and southern Moçambique. Some of the people go into the bush to relieve themselves. Rosa and Mariamu finish their preparations for the departure, carrying their belongings to their 'iron', all the while concerned about the possibility of rain.

Immediately thereafter, everybody starts moving, following the example of the two women. In the cabin of the 1101 locomotive, whose engine has already been running for an hour, Adriano Gil and Celeste Caravela are looking toward the rear through the windows to the conductor's van from where the advance order will emanate.

45

Taiar and his orderly climb into the conductor's van where they are going to sit during the journey.

Let's move, Taiar tells conductor Patrício Joaquim.

From the door of the conductor's van Patrício Joaquim waves the green flag, whose colour is barely visible from the locomotive because of lack of clarity. The train gives a jerk and slowly begins to pull out. Those passengers and soldiers who have dilly-dallied run to the 'irons'.

Immediately after leaving the village and remembering that they are about to pass through an area where he was shot in the leg three years ago, Celeste Caravela begins to pray in a loud voice. *Our Father who art in Heaven, I have ten children. Our Father, I have to return to my family ...*

Adriano Gil is irritated. *Shut up! I want to be able to hear the shooting! You're making more noise than the locomotive!*

It was here!

I know it was here!

Exactly here, at kilometre two seven three! The locomotive derailed and buried its nose in the soil.

I know! I already know! Please shut up! Adriano Gil says in exasperation. *I prefer silence to be able to control my nerves.*

I escaped through the window and, when running, I was shot in the leg, the stoker continues as if his remembering will burn the flesh and his talking will ease the pain. *It wasn't you, it was I! That's why I want to pray. I walked for ten kilometres in the bush, bleeding, and it was only on the third day that I arrived at the hospital, having been given a lift on a bicycle by a railway foreman.*

And on the fourth day, you rose again! says Adriano Gil, sarcastically. *Caravela, I know this story backwards. With your prayer, you're not resolving anything at all. You're only irritating me.*

Yesterday, when you were drowsy, I wasn't irritating you.

I already guessed that you were going to say that as a pretext to bombard me with prayers. A Christian doesn't demand payment for his good deeds. Please, be quiet!

The radio emits a noise and then Seven Ways' unmistakable voice is heard. The commander is talking to the One One Zero One train driver. *Halt! Immediately!*

The train driver speaking. *What's the order, commander¿*

Why stop¿ Adriano Gil asks the stoker in surprise and not a little apprehensive, trying to see what might lie ahead.

Celeste Caravela also does not see anything out of the ordinary and the train continues moving. There is hardly time to react when Adriano Gil sees the dismounted track right there, up in front. He manages to stop the locomotive on the last section that is still intact, thus avoiding a derailment by a metre.

The shooting explodes, coming from the right-hand side of the train. A bullet comes through the open window of the conductor' van and passes a few millimetres above Taiar's head. He changes position and another bullet nearly hits him as another follows and lodges itself near the window. Taiar locates the sniper who is camouflaged up in a tree. He jumps to the side of the train opposite the attack, where the travellers are seeking cover, and sprints to the neighbouring 'iron', which carries the second 'anti-air'. He indicates to the gunner the position of the sniper and the gunner fires a burst of rounds that almost completely prunes the tree and the man at the top.

The shooting becomes more intense on the side of the railway line where the attackers are situated. It is Seven Ways who advances toward the bush in their direction, a few metres in front of his own soldiers, as if this were his personal war. He is on his feet, very upright and without hurrying or looking for cover behind the trees. He has the wildebeest's tail in his hand, a satchel on his back and the whistle in his mouth. The pistol is still in its holster. He lashes the air with the black hair of the tip of the wildebeest's tail and, like one who is driving away flies, so he does with the enemy's bullets.

His soldiers advance, crouching and forming a line, two or three metres from one another, obeying the orders transmitted by the whistle. They shoot and advance in pairs by sections of ten metres in perfect synchronization. Sometimes, Seven Ways waits for the soldiers and, turning his back to the enemy, asks them who has run out of ammunition. To those who have none, he removes a magazine from his satchel and tosses it through an imaginary circle that he draws in the air with the wildebeest's tail and which remains suspended for a few seconds in the smoke as something concrete and visible.

A torrent of insults comes from the enemy.

Soldiers who are sons of whores!

Frelimo's soldiers spoil the women of owners.

Communists!

Cease fire! Seven Ways orders. *They are now fleeing.*

Thieves! shouts one of his soldiers to the opposite side.

Bandits! screams another.

Seven Ways proceeds with some of his men to reconnoitre the sabotage while others search the area for mines. Taiar places advanced pickets in the bush. He walks along the train checking whether there are any dead or wounded among the passengers. He is worried about Rosa, who has been in his dreams during his short periods of sleep the previous night. He finds the nurse who is already prepared. She is dressed in a white uniform that is very clean and is treating a woman who is not seriously wounded but bleeding profusely and crying like a child.

A roll of thunder agitates everyone—they think it is another attack.

Take her to the conductor's van, Taiar tells some of men standing nearby, indicating the injured woman. To Rosa, he says, *You can treat her better there, protected from the rain.*

The lieutenant's order is obeyed and Rosa moves away, followed by the men carrying the wounded woman to the rear of the train.

Taiar turns to Mariamu who is searching for cover under the 'iron', like everybody else.

How did she behave during the attack?

How can I guess, lieutenant? As soon as the attack began, I jumped out and buried my head in the ground like an ostrich. I think she behaved well. As soon as she saw the wounded woman, she fetched her nursing kit.

The lieutenant smiles, as if there is reason to feel proud. Oblivious to the rain which has started falling he makes his way to the locomotive to ascertain whether there is any damage. Despite a few bullet holes the locomotive is functioning perfectly.

I received over the radio an order to stop, says Adriano Gil, amazed. *How is it possible that the commander, being there at the back, could tell that there was sabotage here?*

Don't ask me about such things, Taiar replies. *I also don't know the answers.*

It was God, the stoker concludes.

He isn't a Christian. He's animist, Taiar explains.

He's what? the stoker is surprised. *I don't know that church.*

The lieutenant does not answer as Seven Ways is approaching, back from his reconnaissance.

Some seven hundred metres of the track have been torn up. Two or three days' work, the commander informs the lieutenant. *It's not a recent sabotage. It was done gradually over these last few months. The rails are piled in the bush, about fifty metres from the track. There are landmines around them. All the sleepers have been burned and there's nothing of use.*

Salomão, coming from his train, joins them.

Today, we can work safely. They won't return, Seven Ways states.

Led by their foreman, the railway workers, armed with shovels, picks, screw removers and other steel tools, spread out through the wet bed of the sabotaged track in front of Adriano Gil and Celeste Caravela's locomotive. The rain has stopped and the civilians from the three trains carry sleepers from one of the 'irons'. They will need seven hundred sleepers, each weighing forty-five kilograms. They carry them methodically as the repair of the track and the locomotives slowly progress. For these repairs, it is also necessary to fetch the rails that are piled in the bush when the landmines are deactivated in the direct paths that are demarcated by the soldiers. A few people stay behind for one reason or another. They have been excused from these heavy duties either because of old age, serious illness or advanced pregnancy.

❧ ❧ ❧

I n dispatching the civilians from his train to the work front, Salomão retains a young woman with a child on her back in a *capulana*. The husband wants to know the reason why she is not going to carry sleepers with everyone else.

Is it because of the child? he asks.

I don't give explanations to civilians! snaps Salomão.

The child can stay with someone else. My wife is coming with us!

Salomão violently pushes the man in the direction of the work parties. He shouts at him. *I need this woman here! You go there to the front to carry sleepers or you'll end up being whipped and you still will not see her!*

Defeated, the husband shuffles forward with the others without looking back. If it were at a station, he thinks, he could complain to the stationmaster who always has a voice. In the bush, a soldier is a governor. What can one do? On embarkation, he had known that something like this might happen but the situation had been bad in the city of Nampula where they were living. Recently, their two-year-old child had died and he had also lost his job as a cook working for an expatriate couple. The traditional healer they consulted revealed that dissatisfied ancestors were the source of these difficulties. Because of all this he is now going to Cuamba, his birthplace, to hold a ceremony in honour of the ancestors.

As soon as the man disappears, still thinking that the ancestors have sent him yet another problem, Second Lieutenant Salomão sends the woman to fetch a pot from inside the boat to prepare food for him. Obeying, she enters the boat and he follows her.

Few soldiers move along the trains. The majority are in the bush, in forward positions or on the 'irons' with the 'anti-airs'. Those deactivating the landmines are slowly executing their risky and patience-consuming tasks. Another small group is in among the civilians, urging them in a rough manner that they must hurry in their work and threatening those they consider lazy. At times, they try to interfere with the railway foreman who is responsible for the reconstruction of the track.

It's as if it's done on purpose, Adriano Gil says to Celeste Caravela from his side of the cabin. *They send the worst elements here to trouble the people.*

The trains advance section by section as the track is repaired twelve metres at a time. From the high position of his post, and seeing the multitude under the weight of sleepers and rails, Celeste Caravela thinks about the Egypt of the pharaohs and the construction of the pyramids. He and Adriano Gil rarely leave the locomotive and when they do, it is always to scrutinize what is under the wheels over the next few metres, unsure of the way the rails tremble as new sleepers are never as stable as the old ones.

About a kilometre from them, in the conductor's van at the rear of the third train, Omar Imuli is feeling very lonely with no one to talk to. Only the soldiers in the 'iron' manning the 'anti-air' are nearby, and they talk only among themselves. Omar is half-guarding the line of 1105 wagons to prevent another attempt by the escort to steal the cargo. But he can only cautiously peep through the door or the window since he is wary of meeting a bullet aimed at him and afraid of dying *shetuane*, a non-believer. To drive away the loneliness and foreboding, he occasionally talks to Adriano Gil on the radio asking on the progress of the reconstruction. He also unsuccessfully tries to communicate with the next station, Ribauè.

Why doesn't Ribauè answer? Radio broken down? he asks loudly and takes a sip of the little remaining paw paw firewater just to warm his solitary heart which is full of apprehension.

Taiar's duty is to command the advanced defence group. He is deeply worried about the security of the crowd that is moving from one end to the other, exposed to the enemy's bullets or to the mines as yet undetected. He is with some soldiers on the line, a little ahead of those who are working. From time to time, he probes into the bush or sends some of his soldiers to do so, to relocate the pickets in line with the locomotive's advance. On one of these occasions, he takes the opportunity to go to the conductor's van where Rosa, having been excused from the reconstruction work to treat the wounded, has set up her improvised surgery. There is another woman, almost nine months pregnant, who is travelling in that state because she has had to escape to her parent's home in Cuamba from her husband who is threatening to kill the child as soon as it is born, believing that the father is someone else. The pregnant woman, Amelia, has asked Rosa to stay with her since she is afraid of giving birth on her own during an attack. The nurse has not refused. The conductor's van, besides acting as a ward, also acts as a waiting room. In reality, Rosa feels pleased to have the pregnant woman near her—a life is to be born in the midst of the possibility of death. Taiar gets to know the vicissitudes of pregnancy but is only able to exchange a few formal words with Rosa in the embarrassing presence of the other women.

The work on the track proceeds without interruption, from

nine o'clock in the morning to five in the afternoon when Seven Ways orders a stop. All must gather so that instructions can be issued. With the small axe in his belt and the wildebeest's tail in his hand, he evaluates the work that has been done—a little over two hundred metres has been reconstructed and still he is not satisfied. He vehemently reprimands the foreman.

The latter explains, saying, *The people took a long time to organize themselves. They're not used to this type of work and it's very difficult. Tomorrow, we'll be faster, commander.*

Obstinately, Seven Ways hardens the tone of his voice. *If I get to hear of someone here who has collaborated with the enemy and is purposely delaying the works, I'll not even waste a bullet, I'll kill him with a bayonet.*

The commander then turns to the almost five hundred people gathered in front of the 1101 locomotive. *We'll work from five o'clock at dawn and finish at five in the afternoon. You are all forbidden from moving more than two metres from the trains for any reason other than work or to go to pre-determined areas to relieve yourselves. Women on the left side and men on the right. Anyone who disobeys these orders will receive military punishment because, here, we are in a war situation. There's a water tank on train 1105 and from now onward, those who don't have water can go and collect it from there. There'll be two periods for this—from four to five o'clock in the morning and from five to six o'clock in the evening. You must form an organized queue and you must be careful while drawing water because you will be a target for the enemy.*

W hen the exhausted multitude disperses, Taiar organizes his men for the night guard. After that, he once again goes to the conductor's van but, except for conductor Patrício Joaquim, neither Rosa nor Mariamu and the other women are there. Rosa and Mariamu are cooking near their 'iron' and they are happy when they see Taiar approaching.

It seems as if the lieutenant enjoyed our food, Mariamu says sardonically when he is near.

No, I haven't come to eat but only to converse a little, Taiar says.

Mariamu goes to the water-tank wagon, six hundred metres away, to fetch water in a ten-litre can. Taiar is alone with Rosa, in the only possible way two people can be alone in the midst of hundreds of people always shuffling along a corridor that is only a few metres wide. They sit side by side on the grass with their backs to the bush. The long grass, with the continuous passage of thousands of feet during the day, has transformed into a soft carpet, dried by the sun that shone bright again after the rain.

Mariamu tells me that you were not scared during the shooting, he says.

It's not true! She didn't see anything, Rosa answers modestly. *I was scared, more so than when they attacked the medical post where I used to work and I had to escape by walking thirty kilometres in the bush with all the patients. I think I had more courage then because I was responsible for all those people.*

They continue talking, indifferent to the people who are passing before them, with the usual curiosity of being two beings who barely know each other but who are nevertheless mutually attracted to each other. With questions that are half-discreet and half-playful, Taiar finds out more of her private life—she is single, has never had a serious boyfriend, has no present love affair and is only interested in the profession that occupies all her time.

More discreet, Rosa does not directly ask about love. She asks about the years he spent in the Soviet Union Academy, if it was beautiful or ugly and if the people were kind or not.

There was the good and the bad, just like everywhere else, says Taiar. *And beautiful and ugly places. I used to visit a Ukrainian family, a charming old couple and militant Communists and I had a few local friends. But the situation was not easy; there was too much racism. Once, they threw a pot of hot water at me from the window of a tall building to see whether I would change to white.*

Oh! How horrible!

I don't believe in this thing about friendship among people, Taiar continues. *What counts is the economy, politics ...*

And the friendship among individuals, she adds.

I don't have anything against people in general or against the Russians or Ukrainians in particular. I even had a girlfriend there ... He suddenly stops talking, as if he has inadvertently touched on something sensitive.

You had a Russian girlfriend? The revelation sharpens Rosa's curiosity.

He does not answer. He diverts his eyes to the rear of the train, without seeing anything. Then, he looks her directly in the eyes in a drawn-out silence as if his intense expression were the answer.

Just now, you were asking me so many questions and now that you start talking, you suddenly stop, she complains petulantly. As if she has lost interest, Rosa turns and faces the bush behind her, which impedes her view of the horizon.

Are those mountains still there¿ she asks.

She was not a Russian, she was a Ukrainian, Taiar says. *When I completed the course, we wanted to get married so that we could come together to Moçambique but they stopped us. The chiefs from here and those from there were in agreement. They threatened me with punishment and I, as a soldier, had to obey, to respect discipline. We wrote to each other for some time but, you know, it is difficult for letters to arrive in the bush.*

She doesn't write anymore¿

It ended and I no longer think about it.

How did it finish¿ she persists, anxious. *You no longer like her¿*

You really want to know¿

She nods her head.

We agreed that we'd try once again and get married when the war ended but she married a Russian soldier. She didn't wait for me.

Perhaps the fault may not be hers. It may be the war, Rosa says to console him. *This war doesn't end.*

Yes, perhaps ..., Taiar admits dolefully.

Mariamu returns with the can of water for supper, tea and morning ablutions. *The queue was short. Many people still have water,* she says, trying to justify her not having given them more time to talk. *If the lieutenant so wishes, we can still invite you for supper.*

No, thank you. Taiar rises. *I have to check the pickets before it gets too dark.*

The lieutenant moves away and Mariamu takes his place next to Rosa.

I didn't want to send him away, Mariamu apologizes. *I thought that I'd be helping if I invited him to supper.*

Helping in what? Rosa asks, confused.

Look here, girl! Do you think I'm stupid? Do you think I don't remember Carlitos' looks when he was courting me and didn't I also have the look of a giddy she-goat?

❧ ❧ ❧

At midnight, Taiar comes out of the conductor's van and walks down the train, zigzagging in order to avoid stepping on the people sleeping on the ground. He passes near where Rosa and Mariamu should be but he cannot see them. Certainly, they must be sleeping inside the 'iron', he thinks.

The air around the 'iron' with the first 'anti-air' smells of cannabis, a sign that someone among the guard is still wide awake. Taiar inspects each of the positions in the bush, kicks a guard who is sleeping and returns to the conductor's van for a nap. He finally wakes at three o'clock in the morning and once more inspects all the positions as it is early in the morning, between four and five o'clock, when the enemy usually attacks.

❧ ❧ ❧

Today is Sunday. This is the first thing that Celeste Caravela thinks when he wakes up next to Adriano Gil under the locomotive. He utters the Lord's Prayer, interrupted by the rhythmic roar of the locomotive's engine, in a moderate voice so as not to disturb Adriano Gil who, however, is already up and thinking about a hot cup of tea.

The work starts at dawn at the stipulated time and Seven Ways walks along the improvised quarry, warning everybody, *We're among them! Let us be vigilant while we work.*

Celeste Caravela climbs down from the locomotive as the commander passes. He asks him for permission to comply with his religious obligations, praying with the other worshippers so that they can receive the protection of the Lord.

At the conclusion of today's work, you'll be authorized to meet for prayers, responds Seven Ways.

God bless you, commander, says Celeste Caravela sincerely.

From the tall grass on the side of 1101, a soldier comes half-running and informs Taiar that they have heard the sound of people approaching near the picket position.

They are already here, says Taiar to the soldier on the first 'anti-air'. He sends messengers to the other trains.

The new attack, more intense than the previous day's, does not take long in coming. Snipers, who are perfectly camouflaged in the bush, shoot at the three trains, concentrating more on 1101 around which most of the civilians are located. The advanced pickets return fire for a few seconds and, obeying orders, withdraw to the trains, always shooting, but leaving fields of fire for the 'anti-airs' to perform their pruning tasks. These brief moments allow the passengers and the railway workers to look for cover next to the piles of sleepers and rails which they have been carrying, before the bullets start ricocheting with precision against the 'irons', principally those on which the 'anti-airs' are installed. This is so because the train, unlike the attackers, is very visible from a great distance.

Rosa and the pregnant woman, who is experiencing some pain, are in the conductor's van when the attack erupts. They throw themselves on the floor and crawl to the door. The expectant mother experiences great difficulty in doing so but Rosa coaxes and helps her, exposing herself to the bullets when she stands to assist her charge climb down from the wagon in order for them to crawl to safety.

Lying between the wheels of the 1105 conductor's van, Omar Imuli dreads being captured like a chicken by the attackers. He knows what they normally do when they capture railway employees, having seen many corpses displayed on the tracks—it does not bear contemplating. His confidence is renewed when in the midst of the shooting he hears Seven Ways' whistle. He would like to possess the coolness of his colleague, Damião Pereque. Damião's attitude was admirable when his train, transporting fuel to Malawi, detonated a landmine on the bridge over the Mussankusse River and started burning. Those soldiers constituting the escort who were not killed fled, leaving him alone among the attackers. Isolated from the flames by a few empty wagons, Damião locked himself in the conductor's van and hid under the bed in his cabin. They shot inside but they missed. They tried to break the door and they did not succeed. Someone sent for fuel to set the van alight but all the tanks were on fire. They were about to use a bazooka against the door when somebody announced the discovery of containers filled with Malawian coins that had recently been minted and all the attackers had scrambled away to the loot. The conductor opened the door and ... Omar Imuli sees soldiers passing and he realizes that the shooting has stopped.

On the Mussankusse River, Damião Pereque escaped death by a thread. Omar Imuli has survived once again. Luck will run out one day and he does not want to die *shetuane*. He urgently needs a sip of the paw paw firewater.

Ahead, between the sleepers and the rails, people start moving. Some are more agile and confident while others are slow and cautious. There is a man who does not rise. Curled up like a foetus, he lies, partly sideways and partly facedown. They turn him over. He is a railway worker and was shot in the chest before he had time to crouch into cover. Colleagues and the other passengers gather around the corpse.

Taiar disperses them. *The two of you, carry the dead to the 'iron' and you others, go and work. There's no time for funerals now; they are going to attack again.*

Three wounded civilians are taken to the 1101 conductor's van. One of them is an old man with a bullet that has lodged near his heart. Rosa does not have sufficient skills or the means to attend to the old man who is in a critical state. She requests that the military medical attendant be summoned.

Mariamu has little experience in first aid but she asks permission from Taiar to help Rosa. She goes to the conductor's van with the lieutenant's recommendation that the wounded should be treated outside, as this will represent less risk.

৯৩ ৯৩ ৯৩

The second attack follows, as intense as the previous one. And almost without a pause, only a breath between the one and the other, a third follows. This time, Seven Ways advances with his soldiers behind him, like an impetuous wave that sweeps all before it—so much so that the enemy retreats in disorderly fashion, afraid of a personal confrontation with the Devil himself who seems to be made of air with the bullets having no effect against him whatsoever.

This last attack is deadlier for the occupants of the trains. A group transporting rails from the bush has been isolated during the fighting and four people have been killed and many wounded. The kneaded grass around the 1101 conductor's van becomes a long bed covered with people and blood. Mariamu, who has now been transformed into an assistant nurse, tries to help Rosa in any way she can. The military medical attendant whom Rosa has called for cannot come because he is also very busy. It is rumoured that there are dead soldiers but no one sees the corpses because soldiers do not die. They themselves say so.

Discreetly and without moaning, as if he has accepted that his hour has finally arrived, the old man who has been wounded in the chest dies.

Once the rhythm of the reconstruction has been re-established, Seven Ways goes alone into the bush and disappears in the direction from where the attacks were launched.

The six dead civilians, four men and two women, are covered with their blankets or straw mats and are placed in a line next to the 1101 locomotive. Shallow individual graves are dug about ten metres from the track in a small patch of land that has been stolen from the bush at a great cost. While the graves are being dug, Celeste Caravela and two other men and three women say a few prayers over the bodies and he reads a section of the Bible in a loud voice. Finally, when the corpses are placed in the graves and are being covered with soil, they sing a hymn. The stoker plants a cross made of sticks among the graves and kneels, making a sign of the cross, which his religious companions imitate.

Omar Imuli, who has come to pay homage to the dead, thinks particularly about one of them, unbeknown to all, who might have been Moslem and has ended up being buried with Christian rites. He knows one of the dead, a woman, but because he is still dizzy from the shooting of the 'anti-air' next to the conductor's van, he cannot remember who she is. The other passengers tell him that they do not know her either, only that she had been travelling alone.

Work is resumed at double speed as if the strength of the dead, now no longer needed by them, has been added to the living. Mariamu has to go several times to fetch water for the treatment of the wounded. The soldier guarding the water tank wants to stop her, thinking that she is an opportunist and further threatens her with punishment for showing disrespect to the army. It is only after Taiar's intervention that the situation is resolved when he sends one of his subordinates to accompany her. Even then, the soldier with whom Mariamu has had the misunderstanding reiterates his threats. *You are complicating the matter. A whip does not differentiate between a man and a woman.*

The commander returns in the middle of the afternoon with the information that the enemy has retreated for good. They have abandoned their camp, possibly, because of excessive losses—he has seen a mass grave and plenty of blood along the path that he used. Worried, Omar informs him that he cannot establish radio contact with Ribauè.

Mariamu is also worried. She cannot find her friend who had decided to travel in train 1105. However, she hopes to find her during the afternoon in the 'iron' in which she is travelling.

At the end of the day, they reconstruct a section that is far longer than the previous day's. Freed from his duties in the locomotive, Celeste Caravela reads the Bible to some of the men and women as if he has already established his own church. Rosa is still busy with the wounded that are gathered around the conductor's van. From time to time, she looks sadly at Mariamu who is unusually quiet and preparing food. Mariamu has just returned from 1105 where she has discovered that her friend was one of those killed in the morning's final attack. Carlitos is a living being without a body, she thinks, and her friend, buried in the bush and among unknown people, will be a deceased person without a soul and will never receive the appropriate family homage at her grave.

Adriano Gil and conductor Patrício Joaquim are talking near the locomotive while they wait for Celeste Caravela to join them for supper.

Do you remember? Three years ago, they said there was no war, Adriano Gil comments.

Yes! That there were only a few bandits somewhere around, Patrício Joaquim confirms. *Armed bandits!*

I was in the locomotive when the first attack in this area occurred, against a passenger train, Adriano Gil says. *Lucas Sabão was the conductor. We passed Namina and the station clerk told us there would be problems at kilometre two five one, that there was strange movement there. I asked the conductor, 'Can we go?' He said, 'Yes, we can.' 'Really, can we go?' 'Yes, let's go.' It was during the night and, when descending at Mutivaze and nearing kilometre two five one, I switched off the front headlights and increased speed. We were travelling at fifty to seventy kilometres per hour. Imagine! On that rotten track! When they started shooting, it was too late and they hit the conductor's van. We informed the management about what had happened but they responded saying that there wasn't any war. We continued operating the trains with passengers. In the same place, a little later, there was that serious attack during which many people were killed and the locomotive was burned.*

It was in April 1984, the D-Fifteen, Patrício Joaquim says. *On the same day, they destroyed the D. H.-Two Thirty. After all, there was war. They finally admitted.*

I travelled quite often with the Two Thirty. It was a tough year. Three locomotives were lost.

Yes, also the D-Nineteen in December.

Three militias were travelling at the front in the D-Nineteen and they were the first to die, bullet-ridden. They didn't have the weapons to counter the other's might.

It's true, Patrício Joaquim says and looks at the barrels of the nearby 'anti-air' facing the afternoon sky. He adds, as if talking to himself, *They were not as arrogant as the soldiers. They were friendly to the passengers.*

They were railway workers, like us.

Yes, they were railway workers, Patrício Joaquim agrees.

It is already night when Taiar returns to the conductor's van. Next to his cabin, in addition to the wounded, there are their relatives. Taiar offers his cabin to Rosa to rest but she prefers to stay outside with the wounded and to be with Mariamu who also needs company.

Now that I'm responsible for all these people, I have courage, Rosa states.

Taiar smiles, exhausted and climbs the steps of the conductor's van.

Have you eaten? asks Rosa.

Yes, thank you. I need to sleep, he says and disappears inside the dark interior of the van.

ക ക ക

On the following day, the reconstruction of the track continues without attack as Seven Ways predicted. They advance section by section until, just after eight o'clock, the line stretches firmly ahead in the midst of grass in front of the locomotive. Everyone embarks and the wounded return to their 'irons', except for two who still require attention, so they remain in the conductor's van with Rosa. Mariamu travels in the 'iron' to look after their belongings. At five kilometres per hour, they reach Ribauè at about four o'clock in the afternoon.

As they approach the village, Taiar is in the first 'iron' of the escort carefully scrutinizing the surroundings. He notes that the village is completely deserted, as if it is a ghost village. Not even dogs. Contrary to Namina, where large crowds were waiting for them, there is no one here at the station. Adriano Gil feels his heart turn to ice when he sees the desolate aspect of the station building. Even before the train comes to a stop, everyone already knows what has happened. Doors and windows, including the frames, have been removed. The roof and the walls, covered with offensive graffiti, have been heavily damaged by explosives. Taiar alights with a few soldiers and rapidly concludes that the village was attacked and plundered about three or four days ago and the population had either been kidnapped or had fled to the mountains. There is no sign of the local garrison which was comprised of dozens of men. In the trenches dug next to the station, there is no indication of recent fighting. It appears they fled without offering any resistance.

Everyone disembarks in distressed silence, all insecure and uncertain even of the firmness of the very ground they are stepping on. The rail switches have been sabotaged and the railway workers quickly repair them. The hurried preparations to spend the night keep everyone busy. None think of going too far from the ruins of the station. There is no water in the water-tank wagon and the station borehole has been destroyed with explosives. No one is authorized to go in search of a well in the village so those who still have some of the precious liquid in their buckets share it with the others for them to prepare their meals.

The soldiers who went out on patrol return, bringing along with them a man tied like a goat, his arms immobilized at his sides. They take him inside the station where Seven Ways is sitting. Through the hole that was once a window, Adriano Gil is watching from the cabin of the locomotive. The commander interrogates the prisoner in a rectangle of sunlight that projects shadows onto the wall. Two or three precise questions are asked but receive monosyllabic answers—basically, yes or no. With a sudden and well-aimed blow to the skull, the commander kills the prisoner with his small axe. The train driver is sickened and wants to vomit. He sits on his chair until the nausea passes. He does not tell anyone about what he has just witnessed.

Way behind, in 1103, at the 'iron' with Salomão's boat, the man whose wife Salomão has taken, courageously demands her return. Since they are now back at the station she must prepare a meal for him. High up in the boat, Salomão summons two of his soldiers who are nearby, like dogs around its owner. Though apprehensive, the man does not retreat.

Whip him! Salomão orders. *He'll learn not to interfere!*

Without even being able to see his wife, who is somewhere inside the boat, the man is forced to lie on the ground facedown and with a thick stick is given thirty lashes that are indiscriminately administered to his thighs, buttocks and ribs.

≪ ≪ ≪

Celeste Caravela does not neglect his religious duties, which have now become a daily routine. The faithful who meet to listen to him reading the Bible are growing numerous. Adriano Gil is almost becoming annoyed because, besides performing his stoker duties, Celeste Caravela seems unconcerned about the preparation of meals, as if he were a spirit and no longer flesh.

The man who has just been whipped suspects that he has sustained a fractured rib and, having been told about the presence of Nurse Rosa, stumbles to the 1101 conductor's van to be examined. Rosa notes that nothing has been broken and, on hearing of what has happened, becomes infuriated.

Soldiers are exactly like that, Mariamu tries to calm her. *Salomão's are the worst of the worst.*

Rosa is not satisfied and wants to see action taken against the second lieutenant.

One doesn't react against guns, Mariamu insists. *Be calm, girl. You're not going to change anything but will only attract trouble.*

Taiar appears and Rosa does not say anything to him and he asks what the matter is. She reacts as if she has drunk water with gunpowder and tells him what happened. Agitated, she demands that he should do something. Taiar tells her that he cannot do anything because to punish an officer there and then is impossible. Any condemnatory attitude might result in discontent among Salomão's soldiers, which will definitely affect the mission. Besides, it is not he who must denounce the second lieutenant to the commander but the victim who has been subjected to the violence.

It's easy to say that when you have a gun in your belt, she explodes, using Mariamu's argument. *You're the same as the others, the same as Salomão.*

Offended, Taiar leaves without saying a word. He goes to the front of the train and does not return.

Full of foreboding, nightfall shrouds the trains and the village. Encouraged by Mariamu, Rosa goes in search of Taiar to apologize for having been unfair to him and, with difficulty, she finds him camouflaged next to the trunk of an isolated tree near the station.

They keep silent for some moments, sitting next to each other with their backs to the tree and looking vaguely at the plains that are in darkness and which, to their front, extend up to the Namuli Mountains. Behind these, the sun has long disappeared but they are still visible as if they possess a luminescence of their own.

I'm sorry, Rosa says. *I was nervous and what happened wasn't your fault.*

It's not true, he says. *The fault is also mine. I kill, like all the others. I'm as bad as any of them and I order whippings.*

All of them now kill because they're forced to do so, Rosa insists. *There are the good and the bad in the same way as in Russia, in the Ukraine … as you yourself have said.*

I'm so accustomed to the terrible things I see that I've become used to them and, very soon, I'll become like Salomão or, possibly, worse, Taiar predicts.

Rosa grabs the lieutenant's hand to comfort him and he keeps still for a few seconds as if paralyzed, feeling the contact of the soft skin that is used to healing rather than killing, like his own. He slowly turns and kisses her on the mouth. Surprised, Rosa responds to the kiss and, later, rests her head on his chest. They remain like this for a long time without speaking until she almost falls asleep. Suddenly, she is alert and stands up.

I thought that you were asleep, Taiar says. *I was getting ready to stay in this position until morning.*

I'm going to check on the wounded and the expectant mother, she says. *I suspect we'll soon have a birth.*

෯ ෯ ෯

Taiar sleeps longer than usual and when he eventually comes out of the conductor's van, still before dawn, he notes that in 1105 there are hurried preparations for departure. Seven Ways announces that he is advancing alone in his train up to the quarry that is located about half the distance to Iapala station, thirty-five kilometres ahead. When he sees the look of surprise on the lieutenant's face, the commander adds that he made this decision about ten minutes before, after hearing the singing of a certain bird which should not have been singing at that time. Also, he has had a dream whose significance only became clear when he heard the singing of the bird.

1105 departs. A few dozen people armed with tins, pots and buckets go into the village in search of water, escorted by soldiers. A man, a former resident of the village, tells them that there is always water in the big well next to the administration building. On approaching the well, they all come to a sudden stop, stunned by the stench that fills the air. The soldier in front closes his nose with his fingers, looks inside the well and backs away, nauseated. A few people go to the edge of the well and peep down inside. It is filled with the corpses of the villagers.

Alert, they walk through the village looking for other wells. In the second well, there is a dead dog, swollen like a fat pig. The third seems to be clean and a soldier resolutely takes a sip of the water from a tin.

It tastes different but it's fine, he declares.

They start filling the tins, pots and buckets but, hesitating, they do not quench their thirst, asking themselves why this well had been spared. The response does not take long in coming as the soldier who has had a sip of the water rolls on the ground, writhing in pain. The poisoned soldier is carried away by his comrades and the search is terminated. They will not have water until they arrive at Iapala. If the soldier has died, no one will know since, as a rule, just as it applies in the case of bullets, it also applies to poisoning. A soldier does not die.

But the people are becoming suspicious of the fact that every time the soldiers' violence against them suddenly increases, in an isolated or collective action, it is a sign that there is a death among them.

Irked that there is neither water nor alcohol, Salomão's soldiers ransack the village, carrying anything of value to the 'irons'. Nothing—doors, windows, tables, chairs, zinc sheets, escapes the pillage. They even force the civilians to carry the plunder.

Being accustomed to such occurrences, when Adriano Gil and Patrício Joaquim see the soldiers passing by with the looted goods, they keep quiet, limiting themselves to looking at each other with irony. They are sitting on the station platform leaning against the wall, as not even a bench or a chair has been spared. They have been informed of the man who was whipped because he had wanted his wife back and they comment on the behaviour of the soldiers. Adriano Gil recalls what happened to the administrator of one of the districts of the Niassa Province who was travelling by train.

The administrator was in the conductor's van with his wife and Salomão ordered him to carry sleepers. Despite his position, the administrator found it proper to do as told since his participation would serve to motivate the others to work. Only that the second lieutenant wanted his wife. He expelled the conductor from the van, remaining alone with the wife whom he then raped under the threat of a pistol. The wife informed the husband and, as soon as they arrived in Cuamba, he informed the commander of the Seventh Brigade. Salomão was summoned and, on seeing the administrator, he drew a pistol and, in front of the commander, said that he'd kill anyone who spoke badly of him. Obviously the matter ended there.

And what about that mulatto from Nacala? remembers Patrício

Joaquim, warming to the subject.

Which one?

I don't know his name and it's not that relevant. He's another dead body without a grave. He was travelling with his wife, young and beautiful, and he was suffering from malaria and therefore not fit to lift the sleepers. The soldiers forced him to work and when he refused, they took him to the bush, in that marshy area at kilometre one thirty. They returned without him and they remained with the wife until the end of the journey.

Soldier! Bandit! ... Adriano Gil begins but stops when he sees a shadow projected to his side at the edge of the platform.

Taiar is standing on the threshold without a door at the entrance of the station. From his expression, captured in silhouette, the train driver reckons that he has overheard the conversation. But Taiar's attention is completely on another issue. He has just had an altercation with Salomão's soldiers whom he stopped from taking zinc sheets from the roof of the administration building, which had been left intact by the enemy for lack of porters. He is now expecting the second lieutenant's reaction, which should not be long in coming.

Salomão comes striding toward him, accompanied by a soldier.

Not being able to guess what is going to happen, the 1101 train driver and the conductor remain seated and when they finally realize, it is too late and too dangerous to move. They are transfixed, as if they are not people at all.

You! You don't command my men, says Salomão without preamble.

No, I don't! responds Taiar. *I simply stopped them from looting the administration building. And I'll do it again if necessary.*

Rosa is coming to talk to Taiar about the shortage of water for the wounded but stops at a prudent distance when she sees Salomão. Taiar is standing near the door and, without making it obvious, the soldier accompanying the second lieutenant positions himself behind him at the holed station wall.

My men are authorized to carry away anything they find, Salomão says. *So that nothing is left for the enemy.*

I want to see that written in military regulations, declares the lieutenant.

Regulations are irrelevant here, Salomão retorts.

The soldier behind Taiar cocks his AK-47. Immediately reacting to the noise, the lieutenant agilely turns, with his hand on his Makharov. The soldier lowers the weapon attempting to give a semblance of normality to his action, as if it does not have anything to do with what is happening before him.

Excuse me, lieutenant, the soldier salutes with mock respect and passes in front of Taiar, who lets him pass.

Salomão's sneering smile does not leave any doubt of the soldier's intentions.

Don't play with me, Taiar warns Salomão.

The ire, dissimulated in his voice and gestures, is reflected in the sparks of the lieutenant's eyes.

From the 1101 cabin, Seven Ways' booming voice is heard. *The commander speaking! Ribauè reply!*

Taiar dashes to the locomotive, followed by Salomão. From the platform and through the locomotive's window, he operates the radio. *Lieutenant Taiar speaking. Over!*

I'm at the agreed place. Advance!

With nothing more to say to each other, Taiar and Salomão separate to go prepare their respective trains.

Rosa tries to talk to Taiar. *What happened¿* she asks.

Nothing, Taiar answers curtly.

There, between you and him¿

Nothing. We're about to depart.

How, nothing¿ Tell me. I saw.

But Taiar is already among his soldiers, shouting instructions. Within a few minutes, the trains advance and Ribauè is once again deserted, left to its ghosts.

≪ ≪ ≪

Three kilometres from the village, covered in less than half an hour, made easy by the passage of 1105 and hence no time for sabotage, a shot from a bazooka miraculously misses the 1101 locomotive. It passes above and explodes on the other side of the track among the trees, followed by the chatter of lighter weapons. The train immediately stops and Taiar and his soldiers jump down and start shooting. Frightened and still reeling from the noise of the projectile, Adriano Gil squeezes himself as far as possible between the wheels of the locomotive. He still does not understand how, since his seat is on the opposite side of the door, he managed to get out in front of Celeste Caravela, who is only now calmly emerging, looking for a place to hide.

The first 'anti-air' sustains a stoppage after a few shots and the other is almost useless as it is unsighted behind a curve of the track. The attackers advance, sensing victory.

Assault! Assault! the commander is shouting.

The other train is still far behind and the lieutenant assesses that he can only resist for a few minutes unless he gets reinforcements from Salomão. A worrying thought passes through his head—what if Salomão does not help? The help, announced by a whistle, comes from where he least expects.

No one flees! Seven Ways' imperious voice echoes behind.

Taiar thinks it is impossible! No, from this moment, he believes that nothing is impossible. Seven Ways, who half an hour ago was talking on the radio, is there on his feet with the wildebeest's tail in his hand and a satchel on his back, taking command of the escort.

Seven Ways blows his whistle, bellowing orders and, indifferent to the bullets, he moves to the front, directly toward the enemy who is also advancing. He brings with him the soldiers who, now with renewed determination, were a short while ago on the verge of defeat.

Who doesn't have ammunition? he shouts with his back to the enemy.

I, commander! a soldier shouts, twenty metres from him.

Seven Ways removes an AK-47 magazine from the satchel and throws it to the soldier through the circle that he draws in the air with the wildebeest's tail.

Under the locomotive a surprised Adriano Gil becomes aware that Celeste Caravela, normally a coward and who would be praying in a loud voice and lying prone on the ground, is sitting in front of the nose of the locomotive without any apparent fear and is staring at the fighting.

Caravela, get down! he shouts.

The stoker does not seem to hear. He is absorbed in mysterious visions.

Caravela, are you mad?

Salomão arrives with his soldiers, who run crouching along

the train, and within minutes the attackers are in full retreat. Apart from a slightly wounded soldier and a civilian passenger, there are no casualties.

જી જી જી

Seven Ways travels in Adriano Gil's and Celeste Caravela's locomotive, which starts moving almost immediately, before all have embarked, thus forcing many people to run after the train in confusion. The three trains meet at the quarry and, since they cannot change positions as there are no branch lines, Omar Imuli's and Seven Ways' 1105 proceeds in front for the next fifteen kilometres, a distance they cover in three hours before reaching the village of Iapala.

Almost the whole of the town's population, more than one thousand people, is there waiting for them.

We, those who have managed to arrive, are the nation's heroes—from the Rovuma to Maputo, thinks Adriano Gil.

With exemplary courtesy, Calisto Confiança, the stationmaster and enemy informer, approaches the train.

Did you travel well? he asks Adriano Gil and Celeste Caravela.

More or less, answers Adriano Gil, without being presumptuous.

With God's help, the stoker adds.

Calisto Confiança goes from train to train, greeting the crews. He lives at the station with his wife and three children and, sure of himself, appears to be courageous and cheerful rather than appearing a submissive CFM employee.

Do you know that the Ribauè station has been destroyed? Omar asks him.

In Iapala, we've got a very strong protection force, Calisto Confiança replies.

I'd be scared to sleep here, always in the same place, confesses Adriano Gil.

And with the family! exclaims Patrício Joaquim.

With modesty and skill, Calisto Confiança diverts the conversation to trivial matters. He offers tea to his travelling colleagues. Yes, sir! With sugar! He has firewater for the commander and, seeing him pass by on the platform, offers him the bottle. But Seven Ways, following magical, secret orders, does not drink anything that is offered him by strangers. Happy to have received the goods he has been expecting for so long, the Indian owner of the neighbouring shop and through whom Calisto Confiança passes information on train movements, offers three chickens to the commander. Seven Ways accepts the chickens and, via his orderly, in turn sends one to Taiar, another to Salomão and the third to his cook.

How did he know that we have three commanders? a suspicious Seven Ways asks the Indian shopkeeper.

Because there are three trains, commander, Calisto Confiança quickly intervenes.

While they are having tea in the stationmaster's office, Omar asks him whether there is any information on the state of the track between Iapala and Malema. Calisto Confiança replies and says that one of the linesmen had seen a group of the enemy some days ago.

The linesman himself appears and then assures them that he had seen some movement, it is true, but yesterday and not several days ago. They were many and well armed. Calisto Confiança apologizes for having misinterpreted the information

78

and reiterates that he shares his colleagues' concern for tomorrow's journey.

๙ ๙ ๙

The wounded do not need special treatment and Rosa prefers that, for security reasons, they should disperse among the 'irons'. She, herself, is returning to the 'iron' where Mariamu is. The concern now is water. The station has a small reservoir, but not big enough to fill the water tank on the wagon. The travellers walk through the village with their cans and buckets in search of water. Water is now a commercial commodity, a litre having the same value as a kilogram of salt, which has been in short supply for a long time now. Mariamu manages to obtain forty litres for herself and Rosa.

You'll not have enough salt to sell in Malawi, Rosa comments gratefully.

Not at all. I've got my own reserve for the journey, responds Mariamu generously.

Some of the soldiers of the 1103 escort appear with chickens that have been obtained in the usual manner—'mobilized', as they say. Without the need of force, they bring along with them hungry women who will cook for them and satisfy their sexual needs. The men of the 1101 escort, who eat the soldiers' everyday regulated diet—dried fish and mealie meal—express their dissatisfaction and say that Lieutenant Taiar should be more flexible and allow them to mobilize something, a goat for example, in order to lift their morale.

A 1103 passenger discovers that the cargo wagon carrying his salt has been broken into and that seventeen of his bags have disappeared. He rushes to communicate this to the train's conductor but the latter does not have the courage to face the soldiers alone and therefore asks for help from the chief conductor. Omar Imuli goes in search of Seven Ways who is on the central part of the platform with Lieutenant Taiar, isolated from the crowd of civilians milling about nearby—there is always a requirement for a buffer zone between civilians and the military. The chief conductor informs the commander of what has happened. Seven Ways sends his orderly to accompany him to look for the salt. Omar and the orderly move away, followed by the passenger who is the victim of the theft. In a show of humanity, Taiar expresses to the commander his opinion that the soldiers are being excessive in their treatment of the people. To impress him further, he talks about the principles that guided the guerrillas in their struggle for independence, to which Seven Ways was committed as a young man

It was said that the guerrilla was a fish and the people the water. The water has dried up, Taiar laments. *The people are against the enemy but are also against us—we who are defending them.*

If they're against us, then they're allies of the enemy, Seven Ways warns.

Even when they are against the enemy¿ asks Taiar.

Even then!

The enemy, when attacking us, shouts that the soldiers spoil the women of the owners. Isn't that true¿

A man's a man and a woman's a woman. It's normal that in a month's journey, things like that should happen.

Is it normal to threaten a man with death so that one can take with his wife¿

To threaten is not good. For a female, two males fight.

If one has horns, claws or teeth and the other doesn't, it's not a fight but a massacre. One is a soldier and the other a civilian. One has a gun and the other doesn't.

Persuaded by Taiar's logic, Seven Ways sends for the husband who has been whipped, the wife and Second Lieutenant Salomão.

The three arrive together and, contrary to Taiar's expectation, the husband has no accusations to present—his wife has been returned to him, the matter is closed. Seven Ways wants to know if he has any complaints of ill-treatment and the man answers in the negative, saying that he had only wanted his wife back and now he has her …

The couple is excused and Taiar and Salomão proceed to their trains. Demoralized by the husband's cowardice, Taiar swears to himself never again to defend a civilian and that, one day, he will thrash Salomão if only to wipe that sneer off his face.

ๅ ๅ ๅ

Having obtained his share of firewater, Salomão commemorates his victory over Taiar's connivance. He still has seven years to live, enough time to teach every one of these shit officers how to be a soldier.

In the impoverished village market, Omar Imuli, the conductor, the passenger victim of the theft and the orderly locate soldiers who are exchanging five bags of salt for firewater. They recover the bags after some resistance on the part of the thieves, thanks to the orderly's persuasuve argument that they are acting on Seven Ways' orders. The remaining twelve bags, stolen by other soldiers, cannot be found despite an intensive search in places where alcohol is distilled or sold.

In the enormous expanse of the station, Salomão makes sure that his path crosses Taiar's. *You have defied the law of gravity,* the second lieutenant says.

You were fast and efficient, I admit. You threatened the man with death if he spoke against you.

I don't threaten, I kill. I didn't say I'd kill him, I said I'd kill both of them, husband and wife.

You shame anyone wearing a uniform. If we were not commanders, I'd beat the hell out of you, Salomão. I'm not like this poor husband whom you scare so easily.

Forget about this talk of commanders and officers, Salomão challenges. *If you want, let's go somewhere where no one will see us.*

And you'll bring along your bodyguards so that they can assist you when it's necessary. Isn't that so¿

No one beats me and if one day someone does, he might as well as consider himself dead.

You talk too much about death. When your hour comes, you'll probably shit yourself.

My death is programmed. There's nothing to fear.

Neither of the two alters his voice nor gesticulates aggressively and one who might observe them might think it a civilized conversation between uniformed colleagues. Seven Ways watches them from a distance and, perhaps, it is only he who can guess what is happening.

Much later, Taiar is with Rosa and Mariamu who are cooking the chicken that he has brought to the makeshift camp next to the station. The camp is protected by a wall from the hot wind that again this week blows with agonizing insistence.

Talking didn't serve anything, Taiar laments. *I made a fool of myself.*

The important thing is that you tried, Rosa consoles him.

Obviously, you demonstrated that you're not the same as Salomão, adds Mariamu.

The commander is right; the people have changed. They're no longer the people who fought side by side with the guerrillas during the war against the Portuguese.

It is the situation that has changed, Mariamu rationalizes. *The people are still the same except for the way we now live— one has to hide oneself in a shell like a snail.*

And the present situation is not helpful at all, agrees the lieutenant.

It is nightfall. Soldiers and passengers walk around the village. Apart from the provincial governor's visit some years ago, the village has not witnessed such activity in a long while. The penniless soldiers, with no defined destination, search for alcohol, food or women. The cigarettes they seek have since disappeared, although it is still possible to find raw tobacco. The area is one of the country's major producers. Cannabis is in plentiful supply too. Once their basic needs have been satisfied, the passengers stroll through the dusty streets of the village, more out of curiosity because there is nothing of interest to see. Then they return to the station, worried about their bundles that they have left with a relative or a fellow traveller.

Taiar and Rosa take a gentle walk without looking where they are going—purely for the simple satisfaction of walking together side by side, hardly talking. When they return to the station, they pass near the 1101 conductor's van. Taiar holds her hand, pushes her against the timber side of the wagon and fervently kisses her.

Please stay with me, he begs.

No!

He squeezes her thighs that are full and rigid, glued to the orange and yellow *capulana* and forcefully straightens her against him, slightly drunk from the womanly smell that emanates from her.

Rosa melts in his arms but, with sudden agility, she excuses herself. *I haven't had a bath during these last few days and when I eventually get to be with you, I want to be clean and perfumed.*

I want you as you are.

But I don't want it. I'm a nurse and I've my own funny ways. She prudently moves away from him.

Taiar gives in. *I'll divert a wagon loaded with salt and I'll exchange it for water, sufficient to fill an 'iron' so that you can have a swimming pool.*

If, in order to be with me, you have to be the same as the others, then I'd prefer that not to happen.

You don't understand, Taiar laments. *To steal for love is not a crime.*

You talk of love to every woman who passes you, Rosa taunts him, provoking him. *Even to those Russians who are as white as termites.*

The woman was Ukrainian, he says, smiling. *Ukrainian*, he repeats.

She pounces on the opportunity and moves away, disappearing along the train as the moon and the night form a cloud that is thick and dark.

శ్రీ శ్రీ శ్రీ

At dawn, Taiar has a nightmare and wakes up sweating as if he has malaria. *That's it! This has to happen precisely at this time*, he thinks worriedly without remembering the dream. His temperature is not high and, certainly, it cannot be malaria. The last time he suffered from malaria was five years ago in Yugoslavia when he was on a three-month course and he was saved by an injection of quinine. Thinking aloud, he tells himself that no mosquito is going to put him down!

The stationmaster hands each of the train drivers in their respective locomotives the advance orders duly filled in and signed, a bureaucratic procedure that he does not abandon even during these hard times of the war and even though a journey may only last a few kilometres. He shakes hands with all the crews, bidding them farewell. The trains depart, separated by a few minutes. In his office at the station, Calisto Confiança writes down a message with all the details of the cargo, the number of passengers and soldiers, the weaponry and even the names of the commanders.

They have hardly travelled five of the seventy-five kilometres that separate them from the next station, Malema, when something suddenly appears in the middle of the track, bouncing above the grass. It is something round like a football, but very dark. Not the darkness of the skin, shining and sensual, but the darkness of an empty space, of a well without a bottom and of a sleepless night. Adriano Gil tries to make it out, to give it a name, a category among the objects that he knows and, frightened, he takes his foot off the 'dead-man'. The locomotive slowly comes to a stop.

The stoker screams, *Devils!*

It is he who is the first to identify the object. *A head!* Caravela states, staring fixedly at the gruesome sight.

The head of a monkey? the train driver asks in disbelief.

A man's head impaled on a bamboo stick, the stoker replies.

The nose of the locomotive is only two metres from the human head and Adriano Gil completes the macabre identification.

It's the linesman! The one we talked with in Iapala.

There's a paper on the ground, a message, says the Stoker, preparing to descend.

Don't go. There may be landmines, the train driver warns him.

Taiar and a few soldiers appear, demanding to know the reason for the stop. There are no landmines but there are green flies that are not intimidated by the approaching soldier. They continue buzzing around the linesman's head. On the piece of paper, held down by a stone on top of a sleeper and with drops of fresh blood, is written in very big, well-crafted handwriting: *'Beirut 2 begins here!'* The signature is quite legible—*'Commander Baboon'.*

Celeste Caravela alights and kneels before the head, which a soldier has removed from the bamboo stick and placed on the grass next to the track. He prays in a low voice for that head without a corpse. The soldiers search the surroundings for the body and the limbs, but the search is fruitless as the bush is thick and impenetrable. It is possible that he was killed and beheaded far away from this place.

A railway worker quickly digs a hole near the track and the head disappears into it, unaccompanied by what a few hours before were legs, feet, sexual organs, stomach, thorax, arms, hands and half of his neck, among other things. The last shovel of soil is cast, accompanied by the stoker's pious prayer. Like a cross without arms, the bloody bamboo stick remains planted between the rails.

The tension, provoked by thinking about the fighting to come, transforms Adriano Gil's body into a rigid mechanical mass. His body is almost metallic, a part of the locomotive. Meanwhile, his brain is a hurricane and he feels that he alone, not the locomotive or anything else, is hauling a train of almost one thousand tons and that he has never been so frightened on any of his previous journeys. The picture of the linesman's head challenging the advancing train shakes him more than any of the fire fights he has ever witnessed. It is his own head, that of a railway employee, that is driving him to perform his duties on the track. He mentally repeats the saying that he has heard Omar Imuli saying many times: *A dead animal does not choose the knife*. It is true, he thinks, we are dead animals, without a will of our own. A feeling of confused pride is mixed with fear. Engineers and doctors do not travel along the track but only them—the train drivers, stokers and conductors. The tractor is for the stony road while tourism is for the tarred road. To be on the move, awaiting the inevitable attack that will be directed at him and the locomotive, is worse. He fervently wishes that the world would explode all around him—a landmine, bazooka, a bullet—anything to get the waiting done with. It is a lie! He does not want to be in

Beirut Two. He wants to be at his Number One Home, with his Number One Wife, to sit in the shade of his Number One Mango Tree that is loaded with soft and tasty fruit in his Number One Yard.

It's him! It's him!

Celeste Caravela's shout drags the train driver from the mature mangoes where he has been seeking refuge. The stoker points at a big, dark grey baboon that is slowly crossing the track, thirty metres in front of the locomotive with characteristic nonchalance and a raised curved tail.

Commander Baboon! Celeste Caravela states. *It's him! He transforms himself into a baboon to reconnoitre.*

The baboon saunters into the bush and disappears without showing an interest in the approaching train.

It's not God's creature but Satan's! Go away, evil animal! Go away, you cursed animal! the Stoker screams, staring fixedly at the spot where the baboon disappeared. *In the name of all the Saints, in the name of Christ who sacrificed his life for us, disappear! Go back to the depths of hell! Devils!*

The Devil is not the baboon, it's that smoke! the train driver points, his heart palpitating, at the sight of a dense column of smoke which rises from the bush ahead.

For the next hour they cautiously approach the source of the smoke and discover an enormous bonfire on the line. Adriano Gil instinctively reduces speed as Taiar and a few soldiers jump from the train. Walking quickly, they overtake the locomotive and move away until they disappear into the long grass.

Adriano Gil stops when he sees the soldiers stopped at the edge of a crater that is about ten metres long, dug where there had been a track and a little wider than it. At the bottom of the three-metre-deep crater, three banana trees have been planted, well watered by the summer rains but as fruit, instead of bananas, shells of empty bullets hang from the fronds. It is a demonstration by the enemy that there is no shortage of ammunition; there are also hand grenades and anti-personnel mines strewn about the crater floor.

Beyond the crater, what had previously been a railway track is now an empty bed without rails and sleepers, extending for a long distance. The sleepers are still burning fiercely, piled like a funeral pyre, fifty metres ahead. Carefully arranged, as if the work was performed under the supervision of a strict foreman, the rails are stacked in piles along the track about fifty metres into the bush.

While the soldiers search for mines, Taiar communicates with the commander by radio informing him of the situation. No passenger, crewmember or railway worker is authorized to alight. Seven Ways comes out of the conductor's van and walks along the train toward the front. Everyone's attention is drawn to the bow and arrows he carries, in addition to the traditional small axe and the wildebeest's tail. He walks up to Taiar who is standing in the middle of the track observing a soldier who, ten metres ahead, is deactivating a landmine.

We're among them, the commander says to Taiar almost in a whisper so as not to distract the soldier who is dealing with the explosive.

When the soldier finishes with the landmine, he straightens up and the commander leaves without saying a word, following the bed of the dismounted track on yet another solitary reconnaissance mission.

Celeste Caravela watches from inside the locomotive. *Our*

commander will meet with Baboon.

Which baboon? the train driver asks, inattentive.

Their commander, the stoker explains and with a strange logic adds, *Perhaps they'll resolve the problem between themselves without involving us.*

That would be good, says Adriano Gil. *But one of them will have to die and commanders don't die.*

There's one who died, states the stoker. *One of ours, on the track to Lichinga at kilometre six three seven, if I am not mistaken.*

It's true, it was at kilometre six three seven, agrees the train driver. *But he was the only one.*

I was sitting in the conductor's van, with the window open. He was hit by the first bullet.

The soldiers fled. All of them!

They beheaded him and impaled the head on the track, the same way as the linesman, remembers the stoker. *They stuffed the locomotive with wood so that they could burn it. But they were unsuccessful. The fire went out after they had left.*

It was lucky.

The people in the 'irons' are asking themselves what is happening but do not dare ask the soldiers when they pass by since the military always treat everything as a military secret and distrust anyone who asks questions, easily accusing the curious as being enemy agents.

To chase away his habitual loneliness, Omar Imuli talks over the radio with Adriano Gil. *Why has work not started?* he asks.

They've discovered a second landmine, replies the train driver.

A few minutes later, all are ordered to disembark to carry tools and sleepers. As always, no one is to move away from the track as the area has not been cleared by the military, excepting only where there are rails and where the track is being fixed.

With nothing to do until the crater has been filled in, Adriano Gil and Celeste Caravela help their colleagues up front replacing sleepers and rails. For this, firstly, it is necessary to remove the burnt sleepers from the track, not an easy task owing to the intense heat, which is also emanating from the bonfires burning every hundred metres or so.

The work quickly gains rhythm—fill the crater with soil, compact it and, at the same time, reconstruct the line ahead with the sleepers that are being offloaded from the 'irons' and the rails being retrieved from the bush.

Taiar intercepts Rosa and Mariamu, who resolutely advance, carrying a sleeper. *I'd prefer that you keep your ward in the conductor's van ready*, he says to Rosa.

They have ordered us to carry sleepers.

Well, you are now receiving a counter-order. I want you to go to the conductor's van.

Why? She seems distrustful.

It's going to be bad here, he confides. *I'm not joking.* The tone of his voice does not leave any doubt of the truth of what he is saying.

I want Mariamu to come with me, to help me as she has been doing.

Alright, the two of you can go.

They drop the sleeper and carry their belongings from the 'iron' and then make their way to the conductor's van.

Seven Ways returns four hours later, bringing along with him two AK-47s and a few magazines tucked into his belt together with the small axe and the wildebeest's tail. His subordinates do not ask him how he acquired the weapons—he will as usual give the obvious answer that he captured them from the enemy. But the eyes of the people, fixed on the one who is passing, high and distant as the flight of an eagle, converge directly on the bow and arrows—still the same number of arrows as beforehand as he normally recovers them from the bodies of his victims.

Seven Ways convenes a command meeting, out of hearing of the civilians, with Taiar, Salomão and the other soldiers of rank. He informs them that five kilometres ahead the track has been torn up and that in some places even the ballast has been removed from the bed. They will perhaps spend two weeks here, but it would be wise to do the job in ten days as speed is the key for a successful soldier. At this point, he lowers his voice in a conspiratorial manner as if about to reveal a military secret.

The bandit Baboon, this one who signs papers as a commander, is a fat man dressed in a black uniform with two pistols and grenades hanging from his waist. He wears good boots and whoever kills him can keep them as well as the pistols. They are one hundred and fifty, which means that they are one to two of us. They are well armed—almost all of them have AK-47s. I counted five bazookas, two sixty- and one eighty-mill mortars and three base plates. We're going to encounter a very difficult situation and the commanders must convey an example of courage. Advise your comrades that no one flees. Shoot anyone who does!

During the afternoon, the banana trees that had been planted in the crater disappear, buried by many buckets of soil retrieved from the nearby bush—after careful inspection by the de-mining personnel. Taiar closely monitors the completion of the work. A layer of ballast is laid on the bed of the track and two men alternate using heavy cement and steel blocks to pound the ballast and soil into a compact mass that will withstand the weight of a train. The railway workers replace the sleepers and prepare to fasten the rails. Taiar's mind is on the banana trees that have been buried and will soon degrade to compost.

Having been informed of the extent of the sabotage, Omar Imuli communicates this information to the Iapala and Malema stations, saying that they will remain between kilometres 365 and 371 for a number of days.

Celeste Caravela, in his position in the locomotive, is worried about the burials. He would not like to continue burying the dead so near the tracks. In the future, when the war is over and the railway line has been rehabilitated and the surrounding bush cleared, these temporary marked graves will be profaned by the machines that will unearth the dead from their rest on a false Judgement Day.

In turn, Adriano Gil is anxious to advance with the locomotive as he has the 'dead-man' firmly depressed under his left foot, not relaxing the pressure for a second—if only to feel that he is still alive—both as a train driver and as a man. Before the war, he used to travel at forty or fifty kilometres an hour but nowadays the maximum speed is five. With all the sabotage, these days they only progress three to five hundred metres a day.

They have hardly moved a metre since they stopped. This leaves him nervous, frustrated and feeling impotent in view of the powerful force that keeps the locomotive stationery.

As if his wish has been fulfilled by a muscle-god, population-god or a collective labour-god, the railway foreman announces the 'all clear' for the two hundred metres that have already been rehabilitated beyond the crater. Adriano Gil is now attentive, ready for the slightest advance over the next five kilometres, even twelve metres a time—the length of the two sections of the line that have been repaired.

Rosa and Mariamu stay inside the conductor's van. They have preserved as far as possible the sparse quantities of medication, bandages and cotton wool they still have as well as some tins of water. They are near the door in case of any emergency—they also hide from the attentions of anyone outside who might think they are privileged compared to those who carry sleepers. They also want to avoid giving complicated explanations that they are obeying the lieutenant's orders to soldiers who, being ignorant, might force them to once again carry sleepers.

๛ ๛ ๛

At half past four in the afternoon, as work is expected to finish for the day, Seven Ways orders a stoppage. He raises his hands to the crowd, with palms facing forward, frozen in the air as if a statue of flesh and blood.

Very calmly and without urgency, he says, *Prepare your meals carefully. They are coming.*

Many people, frightened by the announced attack, no longer have the will to cook. They limit themselves to queuing for water and to searching for hiding places under the 'irons' as deep as possible, preferably between the wheels, a place that is disputed by everyone.

Rosa and Mariamu also prefer not to prepare their meal, having been alerted by those coming from the work front. They also go under the conductor's van in search of potential cover.

Accustomed to eating food that is not well prepared quickly, Adriano Gil and Celeste Caravela are busy preparing their meal. To add variation, since they are tired of dried fish, they cook nhemba beans in a blackened pot that is carefully placed on three well-balanced stones, sheltered by the locomotive.

The prolonged, arrogant shout of a baboon, *Iah-huuu!*, is heard above the noise of the locomotive.

It's him! Celeste Caravela reacts excitedly and almost knocks over the pot whose contents he is mixing with a wooden spoon.

Taiar passes by the conductor's van on his way to the front of the train. *Crouch well, Rosa.*

Look after yourself also, she advises. *Don't take any risks like a commander.*

A soldier doesn't die, Taiar states.

Those who are cooking still have their pots on the fire when a mortar bomb explodes a dozen metres from the left-hand side of 1101. Then immediately, small-arms fire starts up, concentrated on the first train—if it is destroyed the other two will be blocked. As with the previous attacks, the advanced pickets near the fighting withdraw. The six 'anti-airs' open fire with the same demolishing force of a herd of elephants. The soldiers who are on the opposite side of the trains also withdraw without exposing their sector so that they can support those involved in the fighting. Mortar bombs lace the sky above the locomotive and explode near the withdrawing soldiers.

When the shooting stops as abruptly as it started, those who were cooking scurry back to their makeshift fireplaces where various pots have overturned, with little of the contents remaining. They try and recover what remains of their food, spoiled now with soil, grass and stones that will not be good for the teeth. They rekindle the fires and place the pots on two or three spare stones, which those who have been forewarned carry in their luggage.

There are no dead or wounded reported. At least, no one has appeared in the conductor's van for treatment by Nurse Rosa. If there are any casualties in the other trains, they will have been treated by the military medical attendants.

Mariamu suggests that they should prepare their supper, but a second attack follows ten minutes later. A projectile from a mortar drops very close to the 1101 locomotive, showering it with shrapnel, soil and stones. Well protected by the steel of the wheels, Adriano Gil and Celeste Caravela are not hit. The stoker starts praying in a loud voice.

The fighting is shorter this time but two men are wounded, not seriously, and a woman is killed. She has relatives on the train, a sister and three children, who assume responsibility for the body.

Dressed in white, and without a speck of dirt in contrast to the dirtiness of the others, Rosa attends to the wounded.

Thirty minutes after the last shot has been fired, as he is going to the 1101 locomotive for his supper with his colleagues, Patrício Joaquim notices blood oozing through the sleeve of his shirt.

This blood¿ Where's it coming from¿ he asks himself loudly.

He runs his hand over his left shoulder under his shirt and it comes out red with fresh blood. Lieutenant Taiar bumps into him and the conductor, panicking, calls to him and asks to be examined.

Taiar feels the shoulder and says, *Something has gone in.*

Gone in?

Yes. A piece of shrapnel or a bullet.

Patrício Joaquim stuffs the index finger of his right hand into the spot indicated by the lieutenant and half the finger disappears inside the flesh until it touches a piece of metal.

It's strange. I'm not feeling any pain, the conductor says.

It's always like that. Very soon, it will come. Go to the medical attendant; he needs to remove what is inside, the lieutenant says. *Thereafter, get some snuff and stick it inside the wound.*

Patrício Joaquim forgets about his meal and goes in search of first aid from the 1101's escort. Without any anaesthetic, besides a glass of paw paw firewater given him by Omar Imuli, he submits to a painful operation to remove the mortar bomb shrapnel from his shoulder. When the wound has been cleaned, with tears in his eyes, the conductor agrees to allow someone to stuff some snuff deep into the hole in his shoulder, the only way to alleviate the pain that will be a constant companion from then onward.

A few dozen metres away from the track, duly accompanied by Celeste Caravela who promises comfort with his prayers, the relatives of the deceased start digging a grave.

Seven Ways goes to the 1105 conductor's van, certain that nothing further will occur this day.

Omar Imuli, careful not to be too indiscreet, tries to sound out the commander on what they may expect. *They let us work but they want to stop us from eating,* he comments.

It's their tactics, Seven Ways responds. *So that we become weak in the body and in the spirit.*

Is it possible that they might appear during breakfast?

They will. It's their tactic. They won't return today.

I t is nightfall. Along the trains, almost no one is moving or talking. Weakened, thirsty and hungry and without a solution for anything, the people lose themselves within themselves and become even more lonely. They are like the living dead, except for the soldiers in the 'irons' with the 'anti-airs'. They are technically 'alive'. Under the 1101 conductor's van, Mariamu is preparing food for three people. The expectant mother feels the child giving her stomach a kick and Rosa, now without her uniform and sitting on a straw mat, lets her thoughts wander while she observes the stars. Only the commanders and the soldiers who are finishing or beginning their guard shifts at the advanced pickets and in the 'irons' with the 'anti-airs', circulate in the darkness. Those who have finished their guard duties immediately fall asleep the moment they lie down—with a remarkable discipline.

At the change of the guard at midnight, Taiar passes near the conductor's van and convinces himself that Rosa is sleeping well in the company of the other two women. The lieutenant hears the unintelligible moans and lamentations from the bodies sleeping on the ground, as if emanating from the bowels of the earth itself, freed from the dark caves of fear because of an oversight on the part of their guardians.

At four o'clock, still very dark, many of people are already up, sitting next to their fires, preparing the food they did not eat the previous day or are heating water to make tea without sugar. They are all on the left-hand side of the trains as the previous attacks were all from the right. Those who carelessly wander to the right immediately feel isolated and return to the others through the wagons with their pots, stones and firewood. Thus, the left-hand side of the trains is a kitchen, more than two metres wide and a kilometre long, with more than three hundred fires and with more light and warmth.

The first bird has not yet chirped and the only sound that can be heard is the metal clinking of pots. Even the children have learned not to cry. All feel dirty and bruised and have slept badly. They have suddenly grown old. They are pallid shadows of what they were a few days ago, their sad thoughts dragged from the darkest part of life.

At half past four, when the first bird starts singing, the enemy attacks again, precisely on the left-hand side of the trains. The enemy rapidly overruns the advanced pickets and forces them to retreat in disarray. Once again, the 'anti-airs' prove insurmountable obstacles for the attackers. At first the guns strike behind the attackers, afraid of hitting their own men. But once corrected, they mow down the advancing enemy soldiers.

The fighting lasts for five minutes and then someone from the bush in the vicinity of 1101 shouts, *Assault! Assault!*

The order spreads a wave of terror among the people crouching under the wagons. Many are ready to disobey the military orders, to submit to the animal instinct of fleeing into the bush, crawling rapidly, indifferent to thorns and stones and, thereafter, running and running while they still have the strength—until they cannot sense any human presence nearby and until they are certain they are alone, as if they are the only habitants of the planet, since the presence of another fugitive scares them.

But the assault order is a false alarm, serving only to disguise the enemy retreat. The people remain crouched for some time, which seems interminable but in reality only a few seconds, to satisfy themselves that the attack is floundering.

Two men and one woman have been wounded as a result of a mortar bomb exploding against a wagon and a third man, caught by surprise, has died. Rosa asks Mariamu to register the identity of anyone who is treated and for what, from then onward in a notebook.

An old woman presents herself before Rosa with her handkerchief full of the leaves of a shrub that she has found and which, according to her, when smeared on a wound, reduce pain and prevent infection. Rosa gladly accepts the contribution as she believes in the efficiency of traditional medicine although she does not understand its secrets.

The 'iron' that has been hit by the projectile is inspected by Adriano Gil and Patrício Joaquim, whose wound does not prevent him from performing his duties. The wagon is badly damaged but can still move and does not need to be disconnected from the train—nor to be removed from the track to become a metal corpse that will gradually suffocate from the bush and rust, like those found along the line up near Lichinga or Entre Lagos.

The dead body is still there, unclaimed, as it does not have friends or relatives on the train willing to take responsibility for the burial. Patrício Joaquim asks some of the railwaymen to deal with the issue.

❧ ❧ ❧

Work begins. The people move with vacant expression and an almost total indifference to the cargo they are carrying, that causes them to bend under its weight. They mechanically obey the railway foreman's orders, whose voice is the only one that can be heard.

During the day Taiar does not have time to see Rosa. He is worried about the security of the work front which spreads out for more than one hundred metres in front of 1101, forcing him in turn to disperse his men over a wider area. But he thinks constantly about her fleshy, tight body and erotic thoughts mix with his military concerns.

In his boat and protected by the other two trains, Salomão can relax and have all the women he wants. He does not always have to employ physical force—at times he takes them with the full blessing of the husbands because there is hunger everywhere. In taking a woman to his kitchen in the 'iron' and to his bed on board the boat, the second lieutenant assures her with promises of food and closes his eyes when she takes something extra for her husband or children to eat. During these occasions, he considers himself a benefactor who gives food to the people like a good leader should—unlike this Taiar who cannot even mobilize a goat for his soldiers in order for them to fulfil their duties for the Motherland.

Toward late afternoon, as the work comes to an end and the trains move for the last time, Taiar still cannot go to the conductor's van since it is the danger hour and he prefers to be near the 1101 locomotive, in the 'iron' with the 'anti-air' where there is no other commander and where, as always, the fighting will be more intense.

Now that the train has completely stopped, some of the wounded and the expectant mother are under the conductor's van. Nearby, relatives mingle and others squat where they have set up their makeshift kitchens. Rosa and Mariamu arrive from the water-tank, where they are given priority in the queue because of their nursing functions. Before they have had time to put down the tins they are carrying on their heads, the first shots are heard, followed by a generalized exchange of fire. They dash between the wheels with the others as Patrício Joaquim joins them.

This time the enemy mortars are not used, probably for lack of ammunition. But a direct shot from a bazooka hits the gunner of the 'anti-air' at the rear of 1103, leaving the weapon in a bad state. Three more attacks follow almost immediately and at short intervals. This time, it is the *xipalapala*, the horn of a bull, which sounds the enemy retreat, adding its contribution to the symphony of the AK-47s, bazookas and machine guns.

At dusk, as the attackers retreat, Seven Ways follows them without wasting time. Only the attentive see for a few seconds his silhouette disappearing in the distance among the trees like the vagabond spirit described in the legends of his birthplace.

It is nightfall; it is very dark and cloudy. Crickets chirp. Rosa is sitting on the steps of the conductor's van and Taiar, standing, is looking up at the sky.

It's only now that the rain is coming, just to fix us, he says.

It won't rain, she replies, not worried.

And if it rains, where are you going to sleep? he asks.

Under the conductor's van, where I've been sleeping as always, she replies.

Mariamu is cooking beneath the conductor's van, very near to where they are and she interrupts. *I'm looking after this girl, lieutenant. It's not going to rain.*

Madam, please do me the favour of not interfering in military matters! smiles the lieutenant, pretending to be serious.

If the conversation were military, kidnapped Carlitos would be a highly ranked officer, Mariamu says jokingly.

The lieutenant laughs, feeling more relaxed for the first time in many days. *A real smile in twenty-four hours of tension is enough to make a fellow feel good,* he concludes thoughtfully.

Everyone along the trains is preparing food, very late compared to a normal day. The escort's food is also delayed and the soldiers, nervous, are protesting to the cook, threatening to throw him into the big pot, which is full of the beans that he is preparing.

Protesting the delay, another soldier belonging to the 1101 escort kicks over a pot that a woman is taking off the fire. *If the soldiers are not eating, then you're also not going to eat!* he shouts.

The husband avoids getting involved in a discussion with the agitated soldier and, as soon as the latter leaves, he goes to Taiar in the conductor's van and produces his military identification card. He was once a soldier and fought against the Rhodesians in the Tete and Manica provinces. He does not tolerate disrespect from another soldier who is still on active service. His wife will now not have time to prepare more food and therefore they will go to sleep hungry. The lieutenant resolves the matter by offering them some of the food being prepared for the soldiers but that they will have to wait, just like the soldier who had kicked over the pot, as it is not yet ready.

ക ക ക

Seven Ways' orderly arrives with a message for the lieutenant, that the commander requests his presence in the 1105 conductor's van. When Taiar enters the commander's cabin, he finds Salomão already there. Omar ostensibly leaves his cabin, which is next to Seven Ways', to show that he is not listening to any of the conversation and he goes to sit by the door out of earshot. The commander tells his subordinates that the situation is dire and needs to be reversed. They cannot accept the routine of fighting during breakfast and supper, thus leaving the initiative with the enemy. The initiative must be theirs. The plan is to advance at dawn and surprise the enemy before he gets into a position to attack. He knows the enemy tactics have been to attack from alternate sides and he does not see any reason why the enemy would change his tactics as he is now complacent and overconfident.

Each one of you must go and gather half of your men, the best, the commander says. *I'll show you the place where you're going to set up the ambush. Ten courageous men who are well positioned are enough to rout the enemy. You know that.*

Commander, the men have not yet eaten, Taiar reminds him.

You have half an hour. Move! Punish the cooks.

Taiar pauses. Salomão, who is already outside the cabin, is waiting for Seven Ways.

Commander, he begins. *What if they don't pass through the ambush? What if they come through another way to the trains?*

I'll take care of the trains, interrupts Seven Ways. *Worry yourselves with the ambush.*

Seven Ways leads the ambush parties into the bush—he leaves Salomão's group on the right-hand side of the trains, about three hundred metres away on a well-worn path next to a small river with very little water. Taiar and his men stay on the opposite side, farther away, in an area where the bush is more open. It is very dark and they experience some difficulty in choosing their positions. But they divide themselves quickly into pairs so that they can sleep in turns. At three o'clock, all of them must be awake.

Taiar sleeps like a rock that has been dropped into the bottom of a well. He changes position on a number of occasions in a nervous sleep that is full of disconnected images, which he cannot remember when he is woken up by the guard at the end of his shift. He only remembers that he dreamed of his maternal grandfather but does not remember about what. What does it signify to dream about one's grandfather in the present circumstances? The old man died over fifteen years ago. Lean, sociable and a fine raconteur, he was valiant but drank too much and was always involved in trouble. Once, when Taiar was ten years old, his grandfather caught a leopard in a trap he had set to catch the wild pigs that were causing havoc in the fields. He approached the trap to kill the animal with his spear. Even with its hind legs caught in the knot of the fence, the feline had attacked and the old man had stumbled. It was Taiar who saved his grandfather from the claws and teeth of the leopard by throwing stones at it as the animal had turned on Taiar who was fortunately beyond its reach. The old man had managed to crawl away, his body looking like a bloodied zebra which a traditional healer took over a month to heal.

Suddenly, the lieutenant wakes and chases away his childhood memories. And what if things do not turn out alright? Despite his magic and competence, Seven Ways is not infallible. On other occasions, the commander has suffered some heavy defeats against forces that were obviously more superior. Just like now! Taiar fears especially for Rosa. He feels more responsibility for her than for the whole train and would not care a fig for it if something were to happen to her. *She is worth sixteen 'irons' and wagons plus a locomotive*, he says to himself. He wants to take her to a place where there is water, where there is perfume and to make love to her. This woman has become his mission in the same way as the Ukrainian was when he fell in love with her and his love had initially not been reciprocated. He had, on that occasion, been defeated when he came back to Moçambique. And now, will he succeed? Now, it is different. Both have Moçambican identity cards, have the same colour, and are on the same train. He feels that Rosa responds to his feelings; she is reacting but in a different manner. She is a woman, a nurse, and does not think as a man, as a soldier.

The six-hundred-metre length of bush that separates them seems to be a thick forest, full of dangerous cats and of men with sharp claws and teeth. From such a distance, with no stones, bullets or anything, he cannot help her. He can only do something for her if the enemy comes through his position and this is what he wants most. But it is only a supposition, among others. He feels impotent and full of anger.

At three in the morning, all the men are up, attentive to the slightest sound. It is the time when the enemy should be approaching. Half past three, four o'clock, nothing happens. Anxious, Taiar is sweating despite the temperature being cool and the light breeze that agitates the leaves. He wants to hear footsteps, to see moving bodies in front of him. But there is nothing. Damn!

Suddenly, he hears shooting, way back and afar. An AK-47, machine guns and a bazooka shooting. Salomão has caught them red-handed, the lieutenant rejoices. Devil of this Seven Ways! Without him, this war might as well be lost!

Although he is confident of the success of Salomão's ambush, Taiar waits for morning before pulling back. The second lieutenant arrives soon after him at the conductor's van where the commander is waiting. Salomão exhibits three AK-47s and a bazooka that have been captured from the enemy who has left behind four dead, two of them with good boots, which he has given to his soldiers. Very excited by his deed, assisted by an excessive intake of gunpowder mixed with the water in his flask, the second lieutenant flashes his identity card to his comrades to remind them that today is his birthday. He is thirty years old and therefore he needs to celebrate. The party has started well with four dead and two good pairs of boots. A jug of firewater made of cane or cashew fruit is what he needs right now. He talks to his men as if able to provide them with everything they need—alcohol, rest and women. He, the celebrant who is all-powerful, merits an award for the successful ambush. They all deserve it! He promises that when the war ends, he will run a brothel inside a conductor's van and he will want all his soldiers there with their penises as strong as bayonets. Soldiers, even those who have been demobilized, will not pay and the civilians will finance the prostitutes on behalf of those who have sacrificed for them all during this war.

Those who have been fighting will be the owners of the women! he assures them with an inflamed pride and drunk from gunpowder and cannabis.

⋘ ⋘ ⋘

It takes a long while to clear—it is misty and colder than usual, which is good for working. All have their tea without sugar, which is not enough. They have seen many people killed or maimed and they feel trapped by destiny. *The next bullet is going to be for me*, each thinks. Several times during the day, they distrustfully scrutinize the bush, thinking they are hearing or seeing something that no one else can hear or see. There are no attacks and they make good progress with the reconstruction of the line. With the respite, there is reason for them to be happy but during the night they nurse ulcers as the mealie meal is heavy on their stomachs and the fish tastes foul—even with a pinch of salt and chilli it is difficult to digest.

Celeste Caravela takes advantage of the calm in order to congregate with the thirty worshippers with whom he prays. According to him, prayer has more force and easily reaches God's ears, the only one who can guide them until final destination. Since God hears well, they pray in low voices so as not to attract the enemy's attention. Adriano Gil is alone preparing their meal, including Patrício Joaquim's, for since his arm has been immobilized, the conductor cannot help. Adriano Gil complains to himself that he has a wife at home, not anyone else's wife, and he has to cook for others. If the stoker does not change his ways and continues to value his stomach over religion, he will prepare food for himself only and force the stoker to fast.

Are you talking to yourself? Patrício Joaquim asks.

Me? Why?

You are gesticulating and shaking your head.

It's nothing. I've only been thinking.

I've just been thinking of what would happen if the escort were to desert us while in the middle of combat. I always fear this might happen one day.

It once happened to me about two years ago. All the soldiers as well as the commanders deserted, except for one soldier armed with a mortar who stayed behind. He continued fighting, firing round after round with his mortar and managed to stop the enemy from invading the train. It was a cargo train with no passengers. We remained, just the two of us. I remember very well when the other soldiers returned, long after the fighting had stopped. He was embarrassed to look at his comrades, avoiding talking to them as if he had been the coward.

And yet it was he who had saved the train.

Yes, it was him, Adriano Gil confirms.

Taiar and Rosa are sitting at the door of the conductor's van, chatting.

At dawn, there in the bush, I was thinking about you, Taiar confesses.

From thinking so much about me, you'll end up being distracted and you'll be shot, she retorts.

I hope that only happens after I've achieved my objective.

What objective? she asks, feigning ignorance.

Come with me, Rosa. Let's go and sleep in the bush.

I'm afraid of snakes and I've already told you, only after I've bathed.

Nurse Rosa! calls the expectant mother who is lying on a straw mat under the conductor's van.

What is it, Amelia?

Relax and be calm. I'm ready but it won't be today.

From the 1103 locomotive, not far away, Salomão's voice reaches them quite clearly. Very drunk and slurring his speech, the second lieutenant is threatening the train driver.

If you complicate things, you'll get into a maneta!

What does it mean 'to get into a maneta'? Rosa asks Taiar.

To die, Taiar explains. *Military language.*

Why does he want to kill the train driver?

I don't know, replies Taiar. *I think if he could, he'd kill everybody.*

The soldiers who are accompanying Salomão persuade him to forget about the train driver and, as he can hardly walk, they practically carry him to the rear of the train. Taiar asks himself how the second lieutenant has managed to acquire the firewater to celebrate his birthday.

Let's go! Salomão shouts. *Let's go be with our women!*

In the morning, there is no sign of the enemy. Seven Ways takes double precautions. *They will come*, he says.

The explosion of a landmine causes everybody to throw themselves to the ground.

It's not an attack! Taiar shouts. *Work continues!*

The man who has stepped on the anti-personnel mine is on the ground, unconscious, with his left leg lacerated, a bloody, pulpy mess. He is a teacher from Mandimba. The soldiers carry him to the military medical attendant. Taiar stays behind and walks around the area of the explosion and the pile of rails, ostensibly to instil courage in the people who refuse to come close.

Irritated, he changes tactics.*You come and carry these rails or you'll be whipped!*

The first man comes forward resignedly because he knows that a soldier does not joke about whips. The others follow suit. Everything reverts to as it was before, as if nothing has happened. At that very moment, there in the middle of the train, the military medical attendant is amputating the teacher's leg. In the wagon that has been transformed into an operating theatre, the attendant uses the last few doses of morphine that he has reserved only for his comrades and those others who are gravely wounded.

Beneath the 1101 conductor's van, Amelia experiences contractions, which are becoming more frequent. Rosa is sitting on the same straw mat that the pregnant woman is lying on. Rosa is dressed in a multi-coloured dress, with blue and yellow flowers. The white uniform that is always clean is on her lap, carefully folded. The nurse's right hand, open like a bird that is delicately poised, gives the impression that it is protecting her virginity. Mariamu is boiling water in a tin pot and arranging clean cloths for the coming baby. The old traditional healer is also present, preparing an infusion of herbs that will make the delivery easier.

Like an aunt who is used to the childbirth of relatives, Rosa tries to calm the expectant mother. *If your child is a boy, he already has a profession*, she says. *You're lucky.*

He'll be a railway worker, Mariamu predicts, always shuffling about but listening to the conversation.

Conductor or train driver, Rosa adds. *Stoker, please no!*

In accordance with Seven Ways' prediction, the attack occurs at midday. Despite the precautions that have been taken, the number of the dead and wounded is considerable, especially among the people working up front.

When the shooting stops the wounded flock to the conductor's van and Rosa finds she is overwhelmed. A group of women form a circular shelter with their *capulanas* open, side by side, to the wind. In the middle of the circle, in the precarious intimacy of a makeshift maternity ward with undulating walls made of coloured cloth and a floor made of straw mats with the sky as the roof, Rosa, Mariamu and the old healer, squatting, deliver the baby. They are not thinking of anything else other than the fact that they are helping a human being into the world in the worst possible circumstances—the one who is born expects peace and here there is only war. The women who stand securing the *capulanas* cannot remain indifferent to the fact that they are an easy target. The attack does not come and the child is born accompanied by insecure smiles of satisfaction.

It's a girl, Amelia! It's a girl! one of them exclaims.

Her name will be Rosa! another states.

No! Those to choose the name are the ancestors, a third one warns. *This cannot be changed otherwise there will be problems.*

After the delivery, Rosa helps the military health attendant treat the wounded civilians. When the last is dealt with, she takes the attendant aside.

Is it true that a soldier doesn't die?

Yes, of course. He doesn't die, he declares. *Look at Commander Seven Ways.*

That one is bullet-proof.

We're all bullet-proof.

And the bandits, do they die? The people believe that they also don't die. Many have seen wounded soldiers but they have never seen a dead bandit.

I've seen many serving as lunch for the hyenas.

The relatives of those who have died arrange the burials in an area near the track designated as a collective cemetery. The sadness is more profound than that experienced at a normal funeral since those who have died will remain here, exiled from the family cemetery—they will not rest or experience the comfort of the periodic ceremonies with alcohol and food. They will not be true ancestors—responsive to the evocations of the living, willing to help in times of difficulty—they will instead become troubled spirits capable of causing harm to their own relatives.

Rosa feels satisfied for having successfully performed her nurse's duties, and for having attended to the childbirth, despite the dead and the wounded. *Trains should carry more expectant mothers so that the number of births will balance the number of the deaths,* she thinks lightly.

I want many children, Taiar says.

Many? Rosa asks, worried.

Yes. Three or, possibly, four.

Oh! Rosa exclaims, relieved. *I thought you wanted something like ten.*

They see a group of soldiers escorting three scantily dressed men. One of the soldiers is carrying half a dozen cassavas that have recently been dug, still red with soil. The soldiers prod the men with the barrels of their guns.

Who are they? Rosa asks Taiar.

Spies or people captured in the bush or in a nearby village.

Are there people who live around here?

They hide in the mountains and sometimes they come down and go to their former fields in search of food.

And if they're unlucky, they meet the soldiers.

Possibly …

From the locomotive, Adriano Gil sees the prisoners being incorporated into the work gang. The locomotive advances a few metres and comes near them. They are forced by the guards to carry heavier loads than the others and at a faster pace, under continual threats of blows. They do not mix with the other men and women who work on the line, being isolated like an island in a sea of hands and feet. They are forced labourers, their gestures are not the same as those of the five hundred men and women who have their objective of reaching a destination, to see their relatives or to buy soft drinks and exchange salt for sugar. Their gestures and efforts have no value whatsoever to the ill-humoured soldiers guarding them, soldiers who regard this duty as extra work and are desirous of ridding themselves of their charges.

Conductor Patrício Joaquim clambers into the locomotive to keep Adriano Gil and Celeste Caravela company. On any other occasion he would also be repairing the track, helping his railway colleagues but now, injured, he is of no value.

Before, people used to stop the train to inform us that there was sabotage ahead, Adriano Gil says. *Now, they flee when a train comes near.*

They helped destroy the track and it's only fair that they must help fix it, argues the conductor.

Those¿ Adriano Gil points at the three prisoners. *They helped¿ They were forced! They're the povo, people who are pushed from pillar to post, forced to do what they don't want to do in the same way as it was during the colonial era. They only want to care for their fields, eat and live in peace. But the colonialists forced them to cultivate cotton, which was not profitable to them. Then independence came and the government forced the people into collective villages, far from their homes, from their burial grounds and from their fields. And then, these others have come from the bush, who kill you if you don't help destroy the line.*

Divine punishment! says Celeste Caravela. *There's too much blood in the land and that's why people don't have peace. It's necessary to hold a very big mass for the whole population to pray together, from the Rovuma to Maputo, and ask for forgiveness for all our sins.*

If that were the solution, I'd pray with you, Patrício Joaquim says.

What sins¿ asks Adriano Gil. *To desire to live in peace, is it a sin¿ Not wanting to know of politics, is it a sin¿ Here, the sin is to be alive, the original sin. These three are lucky. I've been on a journey during which Seven Ways killed four like them with a bayonet in front of everyone. He interrogated them for only two or three minutes and then he decided that they were spies. I saw him recently kill another, in Ribauè. You didn't see him. He killed him with his small axe and he uses it for this. Spies! Povo, yes. People who, when they see the train approaching with soldiers, think that they will have greater security and come down from the mountains to dig some cassavas in their fields. They die because they are hungry and because they believe that the soldiers are there to protect them.*

Toward the end of the afternoon, there is a serious shortage of water—not even a drop comes out of the tap, and no one has any to spare. After having expended so much effort repairing five hundred metres of track, it is frustrating when one has to beg for a glass of water. With their parched throats, the prisoners also ask for some. The soldiers refuse saying that there is nothing

In 1101, the little water still available in the individual reserves comes under military control and is collected in tins and cans under the guard of a soldier, to be rationed and distributed equitably. Those who hide water are punished by being whipped. The soldiers, of course, are overzealous in their searches, molesting people whose belongings they search. If, by chance, instead of water they find firewater, it becomes a cause for celebration. In 1103, the soldiers requisition water in the same manner as they do so women.

Taiar gives Rosa the water that is left in his flask to prepare the meal. Mariamu is in the queue at the water-tank wagon in order to get her entitlement of three litres as well as Rosa's. She demands more for the ward but the soldier denies her saying that each patient must use his or her own supply.

Be careful, it has gunpowder inside, Taiar warns Rosa when she pours the water from the flask into the pot of mealie meal.

She stops, startled.

I'm joking, he says, laughing out loud without noticing that some people are looking at him strangely, censuring him for laughing in the midst of so much distress.

❦ ❦ ❦

At dawn, it is discovered that one of the prisoners has escaped and this raises grumbles among the soldiers. As punishment, the soldier who was on guard is dispatched by Seven Ways to an advanced position, on his own, in the middle of the bush from where he will only return when the journey resumes. With a terse order, the commander declares that the remaining two prisoners must be executed. The soldiers bind them and take them to the bush and, after a short time, return without them, the ropes dangling carelessly over the arms of one of the soldiers—almost as if he has set them free.

When work resumes on the line, fifty people with empty tins and buckets depart, accompanied by ten soldiers toward the stream where Salomão had mounted the ambush. Rosa and Mariamu are among them.

Taiar searches for Rosa but meets only Patrício Joaquim in the conductor's van and Amelia who is breastfeeding the new baby next to the train. Amelia informs him that Rosa has gone to the stream. He climbs onto the 'iron' with the 'anti-air' at the rear of the train and, using binoculars, studies the bush. Intense shooting erupts. It startles him. Without doubt this time, he knows it is the water party who have now been ambushed. And Rosa is there!

Hurriedly, the lieutenant chooses ten men to rescue the water party. Seconds later, people appear from the bush, screaming in panic, running, crouching and stumbling among the trees. The civilians lead the flight, most without their water containers. Then follow the soldiers, retreating, shooting wildly. And among the soldiers is the enemy, also shooting indiscriminately in wild confusion. The 'anti-air' at the front of the train opens fire. Taiar runs to the unprotected side of the train, with the projectiles passing over his head, until he is before the gunner.

He shouts furiously, *Cease fire! You'll face the firing squad! You want to kill our people?*

Surprised by the lieutenant's irrational outburst the gunner stops firing. With a pistol in his hand, Taiar advances into the bush without noticing the second lieutenant behind the gunner, staring at him malevolently.

Taiar runs into the mass of fugitives and, among them, he sees Rosa and Mariamu running side by side about fifty metres from the train. The enemy is forced to withdraw as the 1101 'anti-air' opens up on them. Taiar shoves Rosa to the ground and shoots his pistol aimlessly into the air in an almost adolescent manner to impress her that he is protecting her.

The reason for the ambush spreads quickly among soldiers and civilians alike—the prisoner who escaped is indeed an enemy agent who was aware that they did not have any water, hence the ambush at the stream.

Seven Ways is right when he says that they were spies, says Patrício Joaquim to Adriano Gil in the locomotive as the work re-starts.

And the two who didn't escape¿ the train driver asks.

If one was a spy, then those with him are also spies, the conductor concludes with exaggerated simplicity.

Why didn't they escape then¿

They were probably going to escape later with more information, who knows¿

Ingenious, isn't it¿ They thought they would escape easily, Adriano Gil says ironically. *All of them know who the commanders are, especially Seven Ways. If they had had the opportunity to escape, as it happened with the other, none would have stayed. Those two are the povo, I'm telling you. Believe that!*

You're forgetting how this functions! They force you to go as a spy while they remain behind with your wife and children and they tell you: if you don't bring the information we want, we'll kill your family. They are not heroes, far from that, not politicians or anything. They are forced to come in the same way that all the people in the trains, ourselves included, are forced to travel.

It's easy like that, Adriano Gil says. *Like that, you're justifying everything. We're forced to be born and we're forced to die.*

Rosa and Mariamu are seriously bruised and cut. Their clothes have been torn by thorns and sharp branches. A woman has been wounded in the arm and the man accompanying her to the conductor's van says that he saw another man falling near the stream. The information is confirmed when a woman with a baby on her back searches in the conductor's van for her husband who, earlier on had joined the water party with a premonition that he would come to harm. On hearing that her husband is now a corpse without a grave next to an empty tin, the woman sits on the ground motionless for some time, without listening to what they are saying.

After some time, she says apologetically, *He didn't know how to carry a tin. It's me who should have gone but he wouldn't let me because of the baby.*

ও ও ও

There is now no water on the trains. A soldier from the 'anti-air' escort at the rear of 1105 says he thinks he saw signs of water in the bush, on the opposite side of the stream. Tortured by thirst, Omar Imuli puts aside his feelings of animosity for the military and asks to go with the three soldiers who are willing to look for water.

They walk through bush that is very dense, alert to the inevitable presence of the enemy. He scolds himself for his imprudence. He walks a little behind and they spread out to search the area. It is Omar who locates the stream, barely a trickle. He is forced to dig a hole with his hands in order to accumulate enough water for him to be able to drink.

Ah! The old man has found the water! announces one of the soldiers.

The three rush toward Omar, jostling each other as they roughly shove the conductor, who squats precariously in the narrow space by the streambed.

I'm first! Omar objects. *I'm the one who found the water.*

The soldiers reluctantly agree and wait for him to drink, three times with his hands cupped like a shell. Omar then moves aside to make way for the first soldier. He moves away, among the tangle of overhanging branches, taking a few prudent steps at a time. Upstream, he discovers in the middle of the thread of water, fresh human faeces obstructing the water's passage like a miniature dam. Reacting immediately, he vomits against a tree and then returns alone to the conductor's van, almost running as if fleeing from the soldiers who are accompanying him. In short time he is running a high temperature.

ক্ষ ক্ষ ক্ষ

The afternoon attack that occurs at the termination of work does not result in casualties but worsens the water situation. A burst of firing from an AK-47 perforates the 1101 locomotive's radiator. The red light indicating low water pressure comes on and Adriano Gil immediately switches off the engine.

I'll resolve the problem of the holes, Celeste Caravela declares. *I've done it before.*

After performing the miracle, you must then arrange for about three hundred litres of water to fill the radiator and pray that this shit of a battery has sufficient current, says Adriano Gil in exasperation.

Escorted by soldiers, the stoker and some of the men who worship with him go into the nearby bush. Guided by the stoker, they search for a certain tree whose branches, when broken, release a white liquid that looks like glue. They find it easily enough and return with several small branches. With these they fashion plugs for sealing the holes in the radiator.

Having completed his earthly mission, Celeste Caravela convenes a meeting with the worshippers for evening prayers. There are many of them and Seven Ways orders that they should disperse as he does not want any excessive and unnecessary concentrations of people to tempt the enemy. Despite his religious zeal, Celeste Caravela does not dare contest the commander's order. He prefers to behave like the early Christians who met clandestinely in the catacombs of Rome. But he has an even better solution, without the need to hide—to divide the worshippers into smaller groups of five or six and agree on the prayers and their order—one 'Our Father', three 'Hail Mary's' and one 'I Believe', to be recited in synchrony with the same effect on Divine ears as those prayers uttered in a church.

Omar Imuli is not strong enough to emerge from the conductor's van. The fever aggravates his thirst and he only has firewater to drink as if it were a punishment for his sins.

A soldier temporarily solves his thirst problem by sucking up the water that has accumulated in a hollow of a tree trunk, as if from a soft drink bottle, using a straw from a paw paw tree. Another soldier emerges with wild water melons which, when cooked in pieces in a pot, release a drinkable liquid. Without water, there is no food, no tea and no life.

The soldier whom Taiar sent to reconnoitre the area near the stream confirms that the enemy continues lying in ambush. Together with Seven Ways, the lieutenant adds the final touches to the plan of action. When he passes the 1101 conductor's van, Rosa is already fast asleep.

Noiselessly, at three in the morning, Taiar departs with thirty soldiers in the direction of the enemy who is positioned near the stream. Next to the 1101 conductor's van, one hundred people, among them Rosa and Mariamu, are gathered, clutching their water containers. When Taiar surprises the enemy at dawn in a frontal attack, these people, who are accompanied by a small group of soldiers, are waiting near the stream a few hundred metres upstream. As they hear the first shots, they rush to the water, which is less than a palm deep. There is not enough space for all so they have to fill their containers in turns, an operation that takes time.

No one drinks! a soldier snaps

But he cannot enforce the order as even his fellow soldiers gulp desperately at the water. They don't have much time as Taiar risks being surrounded by forces that are far superior to his. Hardly has the shooting ceased, an indication that the lieutenant has withdrawn, than all those who have not yet filled their containers tumble hastily into the stream, stampeding like a herd of frightened cattle and, in the process, turning the pathetic trickle of water into a useless muddy sludge. At that very moment, having tumbled to the diversion, the enemy begins searching them out along the banks. The escort soldiers start withdrawing, conscious of the importance of the mission and the dozens of lives in their charge. They are followed by the desperate stragglers with their half-full buckets.

Rosa and Mariamu manage to get their cans to the ward. The first three hundred litres carried by the others are destined for the 1101 locomotive's radiator. Those whose containers are not completely full are accused by the soldiers of having diverted the water.

Saboteurs! You won't have anything to drink! a soldier threatens.

It is pointless to explain that there was no time, that the place was narrow and that they had to flee before the enemy arrived because the soldiers who had escorted them are not here to substantiate this and these soldiers receiving the water do not accept explanations from civilians.

The enemy was coming, insists one man who does not want to lose his ration of water.

How do you know that the enemy was coming? a soldier stabs an index finger at his chest, like a bullet for the heart. *You have collaborated with the enemy!*

The man gives up. He no longer wants his water and tries to move away, backing up slowly, discreetly mingling with the crowd—anything to escape that accusing finger.

When the water in the radiator reaches the requisite level, a queue forms for the distribution of the meagre rations—a pittance for the hundreds of passengers on the three trains. As soon as they receive their two litres, they get back to work.

Adriano Gil is freed from his main worry—the locomotive's battery has enough current as the diesel electric engine is functioning once again. The train is hauled forward for a few metres.

Lying prostrate in his cabin, his strength consumed by the fever and diarrhoea, Omar Imuli feels as if he is at his end. He bravely clings to his religion with the intimate conviction that he has finally seen the light.

Patrício Joaquim visits him and Omar announces his radical change in outlook.

Since I'm going to die, either by a bullet or from drinking water with shit, I don't want to die shetuane. I prefer to die like a good Moslem, obeying the Koran.

You'll return to Nampula alive, Patrício Joaquim tries to comfort him.

If I do return, I'll be a good Moslem, says Omar. *Take the firewater that's in my satchel.*

I don't drink. Give it to the soldiers. Not to the second lieutenant's, but to the others.

Okay, I'll give it to Seven Ways' soldiers. It's useless to offer it to

him as he doesn't drink what's offered him. He's prohibited by the
ancestors. He told me so.

৵ ৵ ৵

S alomão is returning to Iapala, a decision taken by Seven
Ways, to fetch water and to evacuate the large numbers
of gravely wounded, among them the teacher who has lost
a leg. The second lieutenant, his soldiers and the 1103 train
crew transfer to Seven Ways' train with the water-tank wagon
attached. The commander and his men transfer to 1103. The
foremost instruction, personally reinforced by Seven Ways, is
not to delay at Iapala as the last remaining sleepers are about to
run out, which means that those on the line behind the trains
will have to be removed and placed in front. If they delay overly,
they face the risk of being separated from the other two trains
and blocked by a section of line without sleepers.

A weakened Omar is the last person to abandon 1105 and he
walks back and forth between the 1103 conductor's van transporting
his belongings. The 1105 passengers divide themselves between
1103 and 1101 as Salomão's train will only take soldiers, the
train crew and the seriously wounded to Iapala.

With the intention of returning at mid-afternoon, 1105
departs at eight o'clock in the morning with its new escort and
train crew. At the same time, standing in for the ailing chief
conductor, Patrício Joaquim communicates by radio to Calisto
Confiança, the Iapala stationmaster, details of the mission and
that the train is on its way. This is a complicated and dangerous
journey that 1105 is undertaking, reversing all the way. The
train is directed from the rear by the conductor in his van, which

is now at the 'front' of the train, and who communicates to the train driver with the regulation red and green flag. On the curves, without visual contact, piloting the train is like flying in the dark without navigation instruments.

The morning passes without incident, as if the enemy has declared a unilateral truce and contrary to expectation, Seven Ways is nervous. He unnecessarily instructs the railway foreman that they must hurry and, as if solitude were a sedative, he decides to settle himself in the boat and leaves orders with his orderly that he must not be disturbed unless there is strong reason for such.

Early in the afternoon, in the 1101 locomotive, Adriano Gil receives a message over the radio from Calisto Confiança that the train has just left the station.

Has it been provided with water? the train driver asks.

Yes, but not completely as we don't have much. Over.

The news spreads and with it hope—everyone is thinking about water. In the two trains, only Rosa and Mariamu have enough water which they need for medical treatment and for the wounded.

At mid-afternoon, according to information transmitted by the conductor, with 1105 halfway back on its return journey, the distant shooting of 'anti-airs' and bazookas signals a bad omen. The silence of the passengers and the railway workers becomes oppressive and Seven Ways, worried, sniffs the air from the deck of the boat, looking for invisible signs that might guide him. Adriano Gil and Patrício Joaquim try to establish contact with 1105 but without success.

The shooting stops a few minutes later and is then followed by a loud explosion followed immediately by a thick column of black smoke rising on the horizon.

The locomotive! Adriano Gil guesses.

It's gone, Celeste Caravela agrees.

A desperate message comes over the radio requesting help for Second Lieutenant Salomão, who is seriously wounded. Celeste Caravela rushes in search of Taiar. The lieutenant asks the radio operator to identify himself. The latter ignores him, repeats his original request and suddenly switches off. The Iapala station tries to re-establish contact but Taiar prevents Adriano Gil from using the radio.

The column of smoke, completely visible, rises high. Seven Ways, much irritated by the turn of events, decides not to attend to the request for help. He is concerned about Baboon's apparent link with the spirits as the latter has managed to surprise Seven Ways several times, constantly changing tactics and adapting himself to the changes Seven Ways tries to impose, as if guided by magical findings. He must reconnoitre more thoroughly. One of these nights he will go to where Baboon sleeps so as to discover his secrets and perhaps succeed in killing him while he is asleep with a silent and well-aimed arrow that has been pre-soaked for several hours in a 'medication' prepared by a Makonde healer.

Rosa, frightened, looks for Taiar and asks what the smoke signifies and whether the other train will make it back. Will they be without water and with fewer soldiers to defend them?

Taiar tries to calm her. *Go to the conductor's van and don't come out from there, Rosa. Even when the situation might appear bad, please stay in the van. In this way, I'll know where you are and be able to protect you.*

How can you when you're always so far away¿

The train is my home. It's where I'm supposed to be. Go and repeat what I've told you to Mariamu.

She gives in, not calm at all.

Taiar joins Seven Ways who, absorbed in his thoughts, only says to him that he must hurry with the work because they are surrounded by bad spirits.

During the afternoon, Salomão arrives on foot, walking along the line with some of his exhausted soldiers. His report to the commander is brief. The locomotive was derailed on the way back, going over with the 'iron' carrying the forward 'anti-air'. Its escort was wiped out resulting in his being isolated at the back of the train with a few surviving soldiers. Worse still, the enemy managed to turn the front 'anti-air' against them and forced him to retreat. Many of his men are dead, though he cannot tell the number, since the train was captured by the enemy. He thinks the crew managed to escape, probably to Iapala, together with some of the soldiers.

Seven Ways listens to the second lieutenant's report and, without comment, orders him and his surviving soldiers to report to Lieutenant Taiar's command in the 1101. The order is a slap in the face for the second lieutenant. But for now there is nothing to do but obey. He has suffered a humiliating defeat despite his proven leadership abilities.

Two more soldiers from the doomed 1105 arrive separately at dusk. One does not have his rifle with him. For this, Salomão orders that he be given ten strokes with the whip. The sentence is carried out right there in front of the civilians who back away, frightened. It is too late for Taiar to intervene, even though he is in command.

When he lost his rifle, he was still under my command.

Salomão's escort has been reduced by half. This infuriates him since it reduces his power, which is already diminished by his subordination to Taiar. In the simple 'iron' that is allocated to him, as he has been dislodged from the boat which is now occupied by Seven Ways, Salomão is like a fish that has bitten the bait of destiny, profoundly affecting his self-confidence. But appearances are deceitful—he will recover and he is very sure of this. He is a poisonous fish that is ready to do anything to recover what is his and even when out of water he is still able to bite. His soldiers, enraged by the defeat they have suffered, and for not having a train of their own with women and stolen salt, take out their fury on the civilians, bullying them without reason and threatening them with death just for looking at them.

The dark wings of night come and many small fires are bright along the trains, more huddled than before because of 1105's absence. Because of the presence of Salomão and his men in 1101, Taiar places a trusted soldier at the conductor's van so that his Rosa is not molested again. Being big, fleshy and pretty and with a face and body that stimulate fantasies, she attracts the soldiers' attentions, especially when she is dressed in her immaculate white uniform. The way she retrieves the uniform from her suitcase bizarrely reminds him of a magician he once saw performing at the Ukrainian Military Academy removing white rabbits from a cardboard box.

The appearance of the 1105 stoker the following day makes

it possible to discover what actually happened. But only his colleagues find out as he does not want any trouble with the soldiers, least of all with Second Lieutenant Salomão. Since Chief Conductor Omar Imuli is sick, he talks with his colleagues Patrício Joaquim, Adriano Gil and Celeste Caravela in the 1101 locomotive. He will, with bureaucratic precision, record everything in his report to CFM—all that he witnessed—but only after the journey when he is safe. At the moment, he hesitates even with his colleagues.

Talk, Adriano Gil insists.

Come on, man. Tell us what happened, Patrício Joaquim encourages him.

The stoker looks furtively out through the locomotive window before he begins his narrative. *On our departure from here, the soldiers that were with us in the locomotive demanded that we move faster. 'I can't,' said the train driver colleague and he showed them the transit form that only allows five kilometres per hour in that zone. 'Oh! So you know this zone very well. You've got friends here? You're collabortaing with the enemy!' said the soldiers. 'It's the transit form that stipulates this, not me,' said our colleague. 'Our mission is not with this form. You complicate our mission!' 'We're travelling in reverse, I can't see.' 'Stop this shit!' a soldier demands.' 'We want to go ahead to reconnoitre.' He stopped. They ordered him to climb down and told him to lie down and whipped him so much he could not sit. He piloted the train standing the whole way. On our way back, when they ordered him to go faster, he obeyed and owing to the speed, we didn't see the sabotaged track. They had loosened the bolts without removing the rails. We derailed and dragged the 'iron' with the 'anti-air' with us. I escaped through the window and I didn't see the train driver. The bullets were like rain. I crawled and crawled*

until I was hidden in the bush, in a place where I could observe
what was happening to the train because I was afraid of coming
out and being caught. They set the locomotive alight and looted all
the cargo wagons. Later, they brought along many people, dressed
in rags and barks of trees, to carry the rice and maize that were in
the wagons. Since there was more than they could carry, those who
didn't have clothes tore the bags open and emptied the contents on
the ground to cover themselves with the bags. I remained where I was
until they went away and then I came out. I avoided going near the
train because of landmines.

The last of the sleepers that the trains are transporting are used and then the greatest sacrifice—a time-consuming, absurd and exhausting task begins by uplifting the line immediately behind the two trains and then transporting the sleepers five hundred metres forward and placing them on the sabotaged section. From now on there is no way back—to reverse even ten metres is not possible. There in front, one kilometre of the track yet to be reconstructed still remains, meaning two or three days of hard work. The people are tired, more so than the soldiers who, except for the fighting, do not perform any tasks demanding physical effort. The people start grumbling in low voices, especially the railway workers. The foreman approaches Patrício Joaquim, since Omar Imuli is still sick and cannot perform his duties, and suggests that he should ask the commander for a midday break.

The commander listens carefully to what Patrício Joaquim is saying. The latter, to reinforce his case, exhibits his wound as a medal. As the conductor finishes, Seven Ways raises his open hands, as if they are his ears for listening to his protective spirits, and announces his irrevocable decision. *There won't be any delays here. It's dangerous. We'll rest in Malema.*

To convince the others to accept the order more readily and without having to admit the complete failure of his argument, Patrício Joaquim embellishes Seven Ways' justification. *The commander has information that we must leave here as soon as possible.*

Whose information is it?

How can I know? From the spirits perhaps and ..., the conductor reinforces his argument, *he has done a reconnaissance*

And then? the foreman asks expectantly.

Reinforcements for the enemy are arriving, the conductor murmurs. *It's a military secret. Don't say a word.*

The news that the enemy is receiving reinforcements in order to attack spreads like fire in dry grass on a windy day and the rhythm of work increases with the motivation of fear.

Rosa asks Taiar whether the news is true.

Who said that? he asks in surprise.

I don't know. Everyone is talking.

It's a rumour!

Inside the boat, on receiving the information from the lieutenant, Seven Ways mutters, *A rumour spread by the enemy!*

There could be an enemy agent among us, ventures the lieutenant.

This Baboon is a rascal, Seven Ways says. *The infiltrator must be caught.*

It's not easy. Everyone is saying the same thing.

But there is one who said it first.

They say it's the commander himself.

The enemy's tactics. We'll catch him.

Late in the afternoon, when work finishes, the sabotaged section of line, although not visible as it is completely covered by the tall grass, is identified by a big tree that serves as a marker.

Seven Ways comments to the lieutenant, *As from this morning, when they attack it will be an all-out attack.*

The people will believe the rumour, the lieutenant reminds him.

Yes, they'll be prepared. We'll suffer fewer casualties.

The following day starts with a white morning shrouded in mist, and without tea since there is no water. The three attacks that occur that day are the most intense attacks to date but, with an obstinate energy, the soldiers resist, inspired by the courageous presence of Seven Ways. He stands tall, distributes ammunition and magazine to his men and draws magical circles in the air with the wildebeest's tail. Along the two trains, thirty metres into the bush, the disciplined soldiers lie in a line shooting back at the enemy, supported by their comrades in the 'irons' with the 'anti-airs'.

No one flees! No one flees! Seven Ways shouts frequently.

Even if they wanted to, positioned as they are, this is not possible anyway. Behind them, there is the iron wall of the trains and among this is the mass of civilians.

Each time the enemy advances on the one flank, Seven Ways is there, revealing himself in the mist. In front of his own soldiers he charges the enemy with no regard for his own safety.

Inevitably the attackers retreat in disarray and Seven Ways incites his men to hurl insults at the fleeing guerrillas.

A chicken eats from the ground! he shouts.

And the soldiers respond in chorus, as if they are well-behaved pupils, *Shoot at the ground!*

Some of them even manage to laugh through their parched throats, stimulated by the smell of gunpowder, by the shouting and by the noise of the shooting.

During the third attack, a little after seven o'clock, Seven Ways' leadership ability is severely tested as the enemy's advance appears unstoppable.

The 'anti-air' at the front of 1101 sustains a stoppage from excessive shooting—the barrel is too hot. Taiar quickly appreciates that without the 'anti-air' their defensive line near the locomotive would soon collapse.

Seven Ways is on the extreme opposite side, at the rear of 1103, exhorting the soldiers who are on the verge of succumbing. With a Makharov in hand, the lieutenant dashes to the locomotive, pursued by bullets ricocheting against the 'irons'. Breathlessly he reaches the desperate men on the ground near the locomotive and struggling against the tide.

He repeats Seven Ways' order, *No one flees!*

The enemy is so close and numerous that Taiar believes he and his soldiers will soon be overrun—that Seven Ways' formula, without him, will not work. He empties his pistol in pure desperation and without any efficiency, only to show his men that he is still there, still fighting. He is more worried about his soldiers than the enemy, sensing that it won't be long before they take flight. It only takes one man to panic and run to induce a mass retreat. He reloads his pistol, ready to shoot the first soldier who tries to flee and he shouts, as one who is crazy.

No one flees! No one flees! he screams.

Because of his shouting, the enemy identify him as the commander and a massive volley of bullets whips the dry ground around him in clouds of dust. Then, as it seems the battle is about to be reduced to hand-to-hand combat, the 'anti-air' resumes its fatal dance and, surprised and demoralized, the enemy retreats.

In view of the determined persistence of the attacks, work does not begin as scheduled the next morning. The soldiers are simply exhausted but now, hardly have they stood up and begun stretching their muscles, than hundreds of men and women emerge as if from inside the earth. They head energetically with unexpected determination toward the work front without waiting for orders and as they walk they gaze at the tree, there in front near the track. This is their target—and free passage.

The wounded gather around the conductor's van and Rosa, even with the help of Mariamu and other women with some experience, cannot do much for them since her water and medical supplies have run out. They can only limit themselves to identifying the more serious cases, sending them to the military health attendant stationed in one of the 'irons'.

Celeste Caravela and some of the worshippers gather the numerous dead near the conductor's van.

Seven Ways is worried and moves back and forth along the

length of the trains, sniffing the air. The reconstruction of the line is progressing rapidly, with all the people having been transformed into a gigantic, efficient machine to carry and affix sleepers and rails. But this does not impress the commander—his mind is elsewhere. He can feel from the air the smell of something that does not please him and, without speaking, transmits this feeling to his subordinates. However, there is no indication that the enemy is going to attack again.

Once the bodies of the civilians who have been killed in the attacks, seven passengers and railway workers, have been gathered together in one place, the pious Celeste Caravela asks permission from the commander to bury the dead farther away from the line this time so that the burial site will not be desecrated by future CFM expansions. Seven Ways authorizes this without reflection, being only concerned about understanding the occult signs that are the cause of his uneasiness.

Those who see the stoker passing, approaching the corpses that are waiting for him, notice something strange in his behaviour.

Seven dead, Seven Ways, Celeste Caravela keeps on repeating in a low voice, playing on the coincidence of the numbers, while he walks.

Led by Celeste Caravela, the members of his church and the relatives carry the dead together with the crosses already prepared to a partially cleared space, dominated by a big tree about fifty metres from the track. A pleasant cemetery, the stoker concludes—these souls will rest in peace. They dig individual graves as this is more Christian and they take turns using the two shovels while Celeste Caravela prays in a loud voice. Without noting any sign of danger, the two soldiers accompanying them become inattentive. The corpses, rolled in straw mats and blankets, are placed gently in the graves.

The two men with shovels wait for Celeste Caravela to finish his words of comfort before closing up the graves with soil. However, as they start shovelling, the shooting begins. The soldiers and mourners alike flee in disorder toward the train. The shovels and the corpses are abandoned in the semi-inaugurated cemetery with the graves open, their occupants exposed to the teeth and beaks of the living.

In his uninterrupted train of worry, Seven Ways distances himself a few metres from the edge of the work front. The explosion of a landmine flings him into the air like a rag doll. Through the cloud of smoke everyone watches as if it were a film in slow motion, with the commander flying and then lying prone on the ground. Stunned, they feel they themselves are falling into a deep chasm of despair.

Without the commander we are lost, is the thinking.

Taiar dashes to the stricken commander with some of his soldiers in tow. The people stop working, paralyzed in collective shock. The soldiers return carrying the commander, who does not show any sign of life. But, strangely enough, those who carry him notice there is no blood on his tattered uniform.

Everyone, back to work! Taiar shouts a number of times in an effort to shake the motionless multitude out of their paralysis. *If you don't work, we'll never get out from here! Let's go! Quick!* he encourages.

Seven Ways recovers consciousness inside the boat and notices that he still clutches the small axe but not the wildebeest's tail. He sends his orderly to look for it and bring it back hidden under his clothes so that no one can see it in strange hands. He does not need to be treated by the military medical attendant, who insists he does. He says he wants to be alone. Seven Ways receives his wildebeest's tail and sleeps with it on his chest, his eyes closed shut. All leave the boat, convinced that this is the last time they will see the commander alive.

છ છ છ

E ncouraged by the nearness of the tree that marks the end of this phase of their suffering, the people continue carrying the sleepers from the rear of the trains, removed from the beds by the railway workers and hand them over to other workers in front who place them in position.

They no longer move with the same vigour and determination of a few hours ago but with a passive acceptance of the last few days. A feeling of insecurity invades both civilians and soldiers. Only those with rank continue to demonstrate that they are masters of themselves, conscious that without their theatrical obstinacy, all will crumble like a bridge that has not been properly constructed under the weight of a train.

The commander has asked to be left to die alone, the soldiers whisper among themselves.

He must be dead by now, the civilians murmur.

The spirits also have a limit, Adriano Gil says to Patrício Joaquim.

Only God doesn't have limits, Celeste Caravela thinks.

Allah is the only way, Omar assures himself, feeling his strength returning after the fever has receded and the diarrhoea has abated.

Rosa states to Mariamu that Taiar is going to manage well

without Seven Ways. Mariamu does not have any doubts in this regard but the problem is with the others who are demoralized by the impending death of the bullet-proof commander who, in the final analysis, was not landmine-proof.

Lost in sinuous thoughts provoked by an excessive intake of cannabis, gunpowder and firewater, whose secrets are known only to him, Salomão waits for the next attack. When it happens, inevitably as it must, he will demonstrate what a commander he is. For now, he must rid himself of Lieutenant Taiar. He refuses to serve under him now that Seven Ways is gone.

Looking hazily at the boat where he plans to reinstall himself, Salomão does not pay proper attention to a vague figure that is moving about on the deck. It is only when the figure descends from the 'iron' that he, in total astonishment, recognizes Seven Ways with the little axe and the wildebeest's tail, dressed in his impeccable uniform, and with his boots gleaming from excessive polishing. Half an hour after the explosion, the commander is walking toward the work front without any sign of injury, with the leg that had stepped on the landmine firmly fixed to the ground to leave the clearly stamped footprint of his life.

Salomão rises quickly and salutes when Seven Ways passes by him looking absolutely normal—perhaps only temporarily inconvenienced by a trivial occurrence. Along the two trains, the people who carry the sleepers, Rosa, Mariamu and the wounded all stop, their eyes wide in amazement, to watch the commander passing.

They murmur exclamations, *A drugged man, indeed! A man of seven magics, seven lives!*

In the nearby bush, the murmur rises in crescendo into a cry of victory, *He's immortal! He's bullet-proof! He's landmine-proof!*

Taiar, busy encouraging the labourers, keeps quiet and turns rigid when he sees the commander approaching. Those working on the line stop and turn, marvelling at the magical recovery of the commander. A woman weeps openly, touched by the miracle. Celeste Caravela drops on his knees inside the locomotive and makes the sign of the cross and pronounces, *Resurrection.*

Like Second Lieutenant Salomão, Taiar stands erect and salutes when the commander stops by his side.

Organize an escort and people to go and search for water, the commander says. *There's thirst all around here.*

The lieutenant obeys mechanically without enquiring as to how they will get to the stream or whether the enemy will be waiting for them. These are trivial details in view of the clear-sightedness of the commander. It is Taiar himself who leads the water party with empty tins and buckets. They reach the stream without difficulty, fill the containers to the brim and, without hurrying, return without covering their tracks.

Late in the afternoon, they are almost done repairing the sabotaged section. Now there is water, more than yesterday, but many people are without food. Celeste Caravela takes his plate of mealie meal and dried fish, settles among the worshippers and solemnly shares his food with them, distributing tiny portions to each, as if through sharing he will reproduce the miracle of the multiplication of the bread and fish that was performed by Christ.

On the morning of the fourteenth day of the journey, ninth on that infernal section of line, the seven corpses remain abandoned in the makeshift cemetery. It is of them that Celeste Caravela is thinking and immediately after tea and having been duly authorized, he makes his way there accompanied by soldiers, the worshippers and the relatives of the dead. Everything seems to be as they left it before their hurried flight. The soldiers, who are marching in front, stop and peep inside the graves. They react in a strange manner.

Oh! Celeste Caravela exclaims when he comes near. He makes the sign of the cross.

The funeral is concluded with prayers and with crosses marking the graves, but the earth is receiving incomplete corpses that do not have ears. During the night the enemy severed each of the corpse's ears, taking them as macabre mementoes, either with the simple aim of terrorizing the people, as an act of vengeance or for witchcraft.

At about ten o'clock, the repair of the damaged five kilometres is complete. The euphoria of having overcome the obstacle gives way to a strange calm, with the people moving slowly, almost as if they have won the right to laziness, as none appear in a hurry to leave. The railway workers calmly gather their tools and the soldiers dilly-dally in their positions. To them, the enemy does not appear to have any further surprises up his sleeve. The reconnaissance patrols have not detected any enemy presence in the immediate surroundings. It is as if the enemy has been swallowed up by the bush or has been transformed into trees or into one of the many bands of baboons that roam the area, thanks to the powers of the commander.

An hour's journey from here, at kilometre two five eight, a new message with Commander Baboon's signature awaits them near the mutilated body of the train driver of the destroyed locomotive. Seven pairs of ears dangle from the prominent branch of a leafless tree. The train driver, captured while still alive, was tied to a cement distance marker and then roasted over a slow fire, with the firewood placed in a circle about a metre from his body. The new message, in the same handwriting and with the same signature as the previous one, reads: *If you pass, you'll only return by air.*

The stoker who had been on the destroyed train nervously inspects his dead colleague. Salomão, who is also present, casts him a long look that is ominous and dangerous and whose significance the stoker understands perfectly. As a result, he seeks refuge in the 1101 locomotive's cabin. The train driver's body is taken to a wagon to be buried later in Malema, which they expect to reach the following day. No one touches the ears that are tied to the tree, fluttering in the breeze like black butterflies on a funeral flight, next to the train that passes slowly and solemnly. Some of the occupants of the trains recognize, with intimate conviction, the ears of a husband, a wife, a travelling companion or of a railway worker.

After two weeks and two days of a honeymoon with death, they finally arrive at Malema. Though they have not announced their arrival over the radio but, being preceded by the noise of the locomotives, they find the whole village concentrated at the station. The first feeling they have on disembarking is one of smallness, in view of the sheer rocky wall that reaches hundreds of metres in altitude a few kilometres behind the village. From the Namuli Mountains, the cradle of the first ancestors of the Makuas, the waters of the Malema River flow, a river that passes through the village and that never runs dry, even during periods of the worst droughts. Malema is land best suited to Virginia tobacco, of its yellowish leaves. In the old days a Rhodesian tobacco specialist used to come and evaluate and classify the crops. There is a shortage of matches because of the war but here tobacco never runs short, neither Virginia, which comes from abandoned plantations, nor *chicaucau*, a strong, black smoke from air-cured peasant crops.

They are going to stay in the village for the rest of the day and tomorrow, a decision taken jointly by Seven Ways and Omar Imuli. It is necessary to examine the locomotives. The chief conductor, who is now completely recovered from his illness, has to contact the local railways branch in order to secure food for the crews, railway workers and the soldiers, a difficult task during these hard times of total impoverishment when CFM, the railways company, is bankrupt.

The soldiers disappear into the village and the wounded are transferred to the local hospital, which lacks amenities but is better than nothing. Rosa also thinks of going to the hospital to beg for medical supplies but Lieutenant Taiar, who has hurriedly, temporarily, excused himself from his duties, intervenes before she leaves.

Rosa, come with me.

Where to?

I'm going to show you the village, the river ...

Rosa looks at Mariamu with a sudden timidity.

Go! Mariamu says.

Does the river have water? Rosa asks Taiar.

This river never runs dry.

Then I'll take my clothes for washing. Do you have any, Mariamu?

I'll go later. I know the place.

There are many people in the river, almost all the travellers are washing clothes and bathing, men and women bashfully separated by a few metres. Taiar and Rosa go upstream, crossing the riverside fields. Rosa is carrying two bundles, one with dirty clothes and the other with clothes for changing into once she has bathed. Taiar holds a small parcel in one hand.

What do you have there? she asks.

Taiar opens his hand. *A scented soap for you.*

Noticing that they are now completely alone, she stops and calls to Taiar, who is walking a few metres ahead. *Let's sit here. I'm afraid.*

You don't have to be afraid when you're with me, he says, stopping.

At this point, behind a big round rock, a rejected piece from the mountain, the river runs deep. There is a warm, clean, sandy place that is hidden from view of those who walk along either of the riverbanks. Taiar leans against the rock facing the river while, behind him, Rosa undresses. Wrapped in a *capulana*, she steps tentatively into the water.

Are there animals here? she asks, fearful.

There are crocodiles. But I'm armed.

Don't be a fool, she says, splashing water at him.

The water is clean and clear. Rosa advances until half her body is in the water and she removes the *capulana*. She ties it around the waist, leaving bare her full, rigid breasts.

You've forgotten the soap, Taiar says. *I'll bring it.*

He hangs his belt with the pistol on a tree, quickly taking off his boots, uniform and underwear and dives into the water with the soap in his hand. He covers the few metres that separate them, noisily like a tank crossing a river. He embraces and kisses her passionately. The *capulana* comes loose and is carried away by the current but gets snagged by an overhanging branch.

Later, after having bathed, they make love and then bathe again, taking full advantage of the opportunity. Once more they make love, and then stretch out side by side on the sand, naked and sleepy on Rosa's *capulana*. The warm sun and the murmuring of the water fill them with a sensation of an intense peace and harmony.

Are you ever afraid? Rosa asks softly, reluctant to disturb such feelings of well-being.

Of course I am. But not in combat, he says with a smile, his facial muscles completely relaxed.

Then when?

When I wake up after a nightmare that I cannot remember. Or when I think about the future that I cannot visualize.

Is it true that you'd like to have three or four children?

Yes, with you!

Probably you'll have the first one soon as I'm in the fertile period.

He looks at her tenderly, pulls her to him and a few seconds later they make love once more.

They only return to the station late in the afternoon with the clothes washed and dry. They are very hungry. There are women who are selling roasted maize cobs and Taiar buys half a dozen. The crowd around the trains has a new smell, no longer that acid odour of sweat and fear—with skin and hair, smelling before of gunpowder and smoke, now pleasantly smelling of soap and even in some cases, of perfume.

Mariamu is very content. She has also been to the river where she washed her clothes and exchanged a little salt for a chicken—a rarity in this village that has been pillaged and plundered by both the enemy and the defenders. She has cooked food, with the three of them in mind.

Thank you, says Taiar, proffering the maize cobs. *They're nice and very soft.*

Your bath has taken a long time, she insinuates.

Rosa pretends not to hear, packing away her clothes.

The water was cold. It took sometime for us to get in, Taiar responds.

Mariamu pretends to believe this so as not to embarrass Rosa. She busies herself with the pot containing the chicken, to which she adds two onions also obtained through the exchange of salt.

Tonight we're going to have a party, she says. *We have chicken and onions. The only thing missing is beer.*

The stoker, Celeste Caravela, can probably convert water into wine, says Taiar.

Rosa spreads a straw mat on the ground and Taiar sits down, with Rosa settling next to him.

They eat their supper almost in silence, smothered by something bigger. Taiar is in love and this frightens him. With a pleasant affection for the world, he feels his responsibility for all those travelling beings increasing, without realizing that the possibility of becoming a father also contributes to his state of spirit. Rosa and even Mariamu are now his family while, over the last ten years, his family has been the army. He knows the train crews' rule that one never travels with relatives as this is unlucky. He does not want to think about it—only to finish eating and take Rosa to his cabin, in the conductor's van.

Rosa is also frightened because she loves a soldier who is in a war, a man who will constantly run the risk of losing his life. It is true, but it is equally certain that in this war anyone, military or civilian, faces the same risk of dying, though the civilians probably face the greater risk.

Come with me to the cabin, Taiar whispers in her ear. *I want you to be my wife, now, from now onward*.

She does not answer but when he finishes eating and goes to the conductor's van, she follows.

They go to the river very early on their second day in Malema and only return later in the morning. During the afternoon, Taiar occupies himself with preparations for the departure while Rosa goes to the hospital to try and secure some medical supplies.

Everyone prepares for the journey. Omar Imuli has bought a few bags of maize, the only thing on sale, and takes them to the grinding mill. Adriano Gil and Celeste Caravela finish inspecting the locomotive, thanks exclusively to Adriano Gil as the stoker is highly agitated and is unskilled in mechanical matters anyway. The stoker is quietly fuming because the local priest expelled him from the village church, together with the worshippers accompanying him as they were trying to celebrate their own service.

On her way back from the hospital with the few medical supplies that she managed to scrounge—cotton wool, bandages and disinfectants, Rosa meets Second Lieutenant Salomão along Malema's main street. In his normal drunken state he grabs her arm in front of everyone.

Does the lieutenant give you chicken to eat? he asks in a loud voice.

Let me go! she protests.

You prostitute! I can give you a goat, if you want. You don't deserve it, but I can.

Rosa manages to free herself by pushing him away and he stumbles and fails to catch her. She is almost running, followed by the second lieutenant's abuse. He is standing unsteadily in the middle of the street, swaying dangerously on his wobbly legs.

You'll be Salomão's wife before this journey ends, you bitch! You're going to be my woman!

Sitting next to Mariamu, Rosa tries to hide her tears when Taiar arrives but he notices. *What has happened?*

She does not answer.

Why are you crying?

Ask Second Lieutenant Salomão, Mariamu snaps, disgusted.

Son of a bitch! Taiar reacts. *What did he do to you?*

Nothing. Don't worry yourself by going.

Where is he?

Drinking somewhere, Mariamu replies.

Taiar leaves angrily, in determined manner, in the direction of the main street. Rosa tries to stop him.

Mariamu discourages her. *Let him be. They are going to resolve this between themselves. They are military.*

Taiar soon finds Salomão drinking in the company of the commander of the local garrison in the only bar that still functions in the village. They are occupying a table that is in the darkest part of the empty room as the only liquor available belongs to the commander. Taiar stops two paces in front of the second lieutenant and calmly says, almost spelling it out for it to be clearly understood, *Don't you ever come near Nurse Rosa again!*

What do you mean by that? Salomão either pretends not to understand or he is so drunk that he has forgotten ever meeting Rosa.

That if you ever come near her again, I'll finish you off! Taiar is almost shouting.

Salomão understands this type of language, even when he suffers from amnesia. He reacts in his usual way. *I'll shoot you!* He draws his pistol but his gesture is slow and clumsy.

With a hard blow, Taiar knocks him down, together with the chair which clatters to the floor. The pistol rolls away and the lieutenant grabs it.

You can get it back from Commander Seven Ways.

The commander of the local garrison tries to intervene but Taiar stops him. *Don't involve yourself; this is a personal matter.*

Taiar leaves with the Second Lieutenant's pistol. Salomão rises with some difficulty and wipes his hand over his mouth, which is dirty with blood. He looks for his glass but it is broken.

I want a glass! he screams at the waiter.

T hat night Taiar and Rosa retire early to the cabin, chatting until late about their lives and their dreams. Taiar confesses that until he met her he had had no plans for the future, except for a vague desire to study in order to have a civilian profession.

When the war ends, it is then that I'll make plans. That's what I used to think. Why make plans if I'm going to die the next day? It was a waste of time! But now, it's different. I'm to even think about what I'm going to do next week. I have you and, probably, you're going to have a baby.

Yes, it's necessary to think and plan. You're going to be in one place while I'll be in another.

If we get married, one of us can get a transfer.

It'll take years. Perhaps, it would be easier if the war was to finish earlier. You know how the government bureaucracies are.

You can stop working.

And survive on what you earn?

You see, already complaining that I'm earning too little. You already sound like an old woman, nagging her husband because of money.

Rosa laughs, embraces him and buries her face in his shoulder.

Then Taiar realizes, she is crying. *Hey! What is it I've said?*

Nothing. I got sad when I realized that we don't have any place that's our home. It's a train and I wish I had known you in another place, under different circumstances. Here, I'm scared of everything, more so now than at any other time. I'm scared of this man, the second lieutenant.

That one's a coward, Taiar interrupts. *Unarmed, he doesn't threaten anyone. Without a weapon, he is nothing.*

But he's got a weapon.

Don't think anymore about him, Rosa. It's a bad thing to think before one sleeps.

When I was young, I used to be scared of dying at night, while asleep.

One dies while sleeping, he says, joking. *But, generally, it's people who are old, without a morning.*

I used to think that if one died while asleep, death would be darker than if it occurred during the day.

There's no clarity in death. During the day or at night, it's only darkness. You close your eyes and that's it.

You're inventing stories. How do you know? Don't you believe in God?

God? God? he asks himself as if trying to remember. *I think I know him but I can't put a name to the face.*

She laughs against her will as she does not find anything funny about being disrespectful to God.

He yawns and moves from her, sleeping on the narrow, hard bed on the opposite side of the cabin. *It's almost time to wake up*, he says. *Goodnight, my darling.*

The distance to the next station, Mutuali, is fifty kilometres. Meanwhile, Seven Ways knows that all will be decided during the first few kilometres of this phase, a sector that is still within reach of Baboon's group. There are no special precautions to take but only to proceed and see what will happen—and to react accordingly.

Taiar is on the front part of the train, in the 'iron' carrying the 'anti-air'. Rosa, Mariamu, Amelia with the baby and some of the wounded are travelling in the conductor's van with Conductor Patrício Joaquim, while Salomão is in the 'iron' with the second 'anti-air'. His men and Taiar's are mixed together in the two 'irons'.

Just after leaving the village, on a steep rise, with the track covered in grass that is wet from the mist, 1101 gradually reduces speed until it completely stops. For a fraction of a second, the train is stationery and then starts sliding backward despite the locomotive's efforts and the wheels skid, failing to grip the rails. The stoker, worried, glances out through the window at the train not far behind—Seven Ways had decided to reduce the distance between the trains. The stoker cannot see the other train because of the curve of the track. When Adriano Gil eventually manages to stop the train, the soldiers alight and run forward, some threatening him for being a saboteur—that he collaborates with the enemy. They order him to advance.

Taiar, who had momentarily moved forward to reconnoitre the track ahead, intervenes and saves Adriano Gil from suffering some terrible consequences as a result of the locomotive's skidding.

It's not the train driver's fault. Taiar calms the soldiers. *It's uphill and the track is wet and covered with grass. The locomotive is skidding. Nothing more.*

The locomotive's sandbag mechanism that releases sand onto the rails for better grip has not functioned for a long time because of a shortage of spare parts. The solution is a rudimentary method known to all who travel the line.

Accompanied by an escort, the railway workers walk in front, collecting small stones and placing them on the two rails, five centimetres apart. Thus the train advances on the stones as if it had cogwheels, and manages to reach the top of the rise from where an immense plain can be seen covered by trees and grass that is taller than a man.

While progressing through a grassy area covering the track, Adriano Gil and Celeste Caravela cannot see anything. Suddenly, the locomotive shudders and they see ahead the two rails separating from each other, as if they are large serpents, disconnected and freed from the sleepers. Thanks to the slow speed at which they are travelling as well as Adriano Gil's quick thinking and reactionary skill, the locomotive manages to stay on the rails with the engine still running, although the front six wheels are spinning in the air off the rails. Almost immediately, before anyone manages to jump down and seek cover under the wagons, shooting erupts, resulting in many immediate casualties.

The enemy is shooting from five metres, completely concealed in the grass, and if any are killed, no one can see. Trapped in the 'irons' the passengers lie flat but the soldiers have to stand in order to shoot and thus many are shot from almost point-blank range. Because of the closeness of the enemy, the 'anti-airs' are useless as they cannot depress and they therefore overshoot their targets.

Grenades are thrown and begin to explode near Salomão's 'iron'. With bullets pursuing him like a swarm of bees, Taiar tries with the help of the gunner to alter the elevation of the 'anti-air' in order to be able to at least shoot toward the rear of the wagon that is under greatest threat. At a glance, he notices men running to the conductor's van where Rosa is and his heart explodes.

All the occupants of the conductor's van are lying on the floor, protected from the shooting, but the door is invitingly open. When Rosa becomes aware of the danger, she dashes to close the door, exposing herself to the bullets that scream through the open windows. Hardly has she managed to close the door than there is somebody trying to knock it down from the outside.

At various points along the trains, the enemy soldiers approach the wagons, raise their rifles over the sides and shoot inside without seeing their targets. Grenades continue to explode around the escort's 'iron' at the rear of 1101. With the 'anti-air' elevation corrected and now pointing backward almost level with the train, Taiar himself opens fire above the nearest wagons, risking hitting his own people. He hits the grass near the 'iron' that is about to be overrun by the enemy, as if he were harvesting wheat. At the last moment he manages to hit the fat enemy soldier with the black uniform and two pistols in the waist who is running toward the wagon with a grenade in his hand, only seconds away from throwing the bomb into the defenceless wagon.

They've killed the commander! an enemy voice shouts from the grass. *They've killed the commander!*

Fighting continues for a few seconds at the extremities of the trains until the news spreads. Then the enemy's guns become silent. A few shots still sound out but from afar, announcing the enemy retreat. Taiar leaves the 'anti-air' to the gunner and jumps to the ground, running with soldiers who are galvanized by the unexpected victory. They advance for several metres into the grass, shooting at the disappearing figures. In a few moments the firing from the wagons also ceases as it becomes clear that the enemy has retreated in absolute disarray.

As the fighting comes to a close, Rosa tries to catch a glimpse of what is happening up front where there is great agitation. She has a feeling that a tragedy is unfolding when she sees a group of soldiers carrying a uniformed body. She stands motionless, without reacting. One of the soldiers pushes her roughly aside so that they can bring in the lieutenant who has been gravely wounded by a bullet in the back. The military medical attendant is quickly summoned and the soldiers stop Rosa from entering the conductor's van, chasing everyone out, including the legitimate occupant, the conductor. Furious at what has happened to their lieutenant the soldiers drag Baboon's body by the legs and tie it to the front of the locomotive.

The railway workers prepare to lift the front part of the one-hundred-and-twenty-ton locomotive, using four fifty-ton jacks to tighten the rails underneath and then to lift the first wheel onto the rail. They do this in front of the shredded corpse of the enemy commander.

When Taiar, weak from loss of blood, regains consciousness, his first thought is of Rosa. *Where's my wife?* he asks. *Call her.*

It is only then that they allow Rosa in. She has been treating the wounded, not wanting to confront her own reality.

Having been informed that the lieutenant has been shot in the back, Seven Ways interrogates the soldiers who had stayed behind in the 'iron' when Taiar had jumped out. One of Salomão's soldiers says that he saw him falling when he turned toward the train to give an order. Otherwise, no one else saw the lieutenant being shot because of the confusion at the time. The enquiry is suspended to be resumed upon arrival at the headquarters in Nampula.

Taiar is entitled to Commander Baboon's boots as well as the one pistol, since the other was smashed into pieces by the impact of the shell from the 'anti-air'. Seven Ways sends his orderly to present these things to the lieutenant, almost like an awards ceremony.

෧ ෧ ෧

That night, with the labours of getting the locomotive back onto the rails temporarily suspended, Celeste Caravela remains for some time in front of the locomotive, where the enemy commander's corpse is still tied. Without attracting anybody's attention, he silently obeys secret guidelines known only to him and, soon thereafter, he goes from 'iron' to 'iron', exhibiting the heart that he has removed from Commander Baboon's chest. The soldiers laugh noisily when they realize what is happening while the civilians, horrified, look away.

God gives and God takes, Celeste Caravela repeats over and over in a soft, monotonous voice. *They've been saying that a bandit doesn't die. Of course he does. Look. He is also God's creature.*

It is only Omar Imuli, in his capacity as chief conductor, who persuades the stoker to let go of the bloody piece of muscle.

Much later, now very calm and leaning against the wheels of the locomotive, he talks to the worshippers about the apocalypse that has befallen this land which is inundated with blood and which only fire can purify.

∽ ∽ ∽

The bullet, which has lodged itself close to Taiar's heart, is still there and the military medical attendant cannot do anything about it. On the following day, after a night that he did not feel passing, the lieutenant breathes with difficulty. Besides watching over him, Rosa has had to attend to the wounded by the light of a fire.

Taiar talks to her slowly and in a low voice, trying to save his strength. *What irks me is that I've been shot in the back and they'll think that I was running away.*

Everyone knows that it is you who saved us, says Rosa consoling him.

Toward late morning, the locomotive is at last back on the rails and the journey continues to Mutuali, a village without resources, where they spend the night. There is no way of evacuating Taiar from here, nor any of the other wounded. Therefore they have to proceed to Cuamba where there is a hospital that is relatively well equipped and staffed by Russian and Bulgarian doctors.

Taiar talks less, semi-delirious. *We've been drugged by a big witch, all drugged to kill one another,* he complains. *What's the use of being lucid before dying, knowing that throughout my life, I never did what I've always wanted to do? I've dreamed of rearing cattle, looking after the fields and I've always thought of living in the rural areas, now and then hunting with a bow and arrow like my grandfather. But I've only managed to make war, hunting men.*

Isn't that sad? By any chance, is it fair?

The Mutuali stationmaster gives the advance order, adding that they will have free passage to Cuamba, fifty-four kilometres away, a distance they will cover in ten hours.

At sunset they approach Cuamba. Taiar is very weak, lying down with his head supported in Rosa's lap.

I can see the Metucue Mountain, she says. *When the war ends, we'll go up there. It's only sixteen kilometres from the village.*

You will go alone, Taiar says.

With our son, she says and begins to cry softly.

Yes, take him there. Show him from up there the railway line where we got to know each other.

I'll take him, she promises in a halting voice.

I can't see the mountain lying like this. Taiar's voice is a dry river in which the last thread of life runs. *Help me rise. I want to see it.*

She props up him by the shoulders and he half-sits with his back resting on her chest, looking out of the window.

I can see it, he says. *It is very bright. Everything is clear. So bright … as if we live in the sun. I can see many suns.*

Almost smiling, he closes his eyes and, motionless, does not open them again. Rosa puts his head on her lap once again. She continues to cry softly and her tears fall on Taiar's serene face. She is startled, as if she has been sleeping, by the train driver hooting on the outskirts of the town of Cuamba.

⊷ ⊷ ⊷

Adriano Gil is accompanied in the locomotive by the 1103 stoker as Celeste Caravela has completely lost his mental faculty and is travelling in an 'iron' where he proclaims his visions of the apocalypse to the enraptured worshippers at his feet.

This time, it is not the locomotives that attract the crowds alongside the track. All eyes are fixed on Commander Baboon's mutilated body without a heart, tied to the nose of the locomotive. Gradually, more and more people gather and start moving with the locomotive. A collective roar rises when someone throws the first stone. Then, many others pound the locomotive with stones, aiming at the corpse.

A soldier from the first 'iron' fires a volley of bullets into the air and, like water spreading in front of the prow of a ship, the multitude disperses and the stoning ceases.

... fim ...